The maharani peered again into the darkness. She thought she saw a dark shadow move across the passage, but it might have been a trick of her weak eyes. She did not believe the stories of these pale English ghosts the maids had been speaking of. The ladies who served her were far more sensible. She moved forward, intent on reaching the dark-paneled sitting room with its strange white columns at the end of the passageway.

She heard the rustle of fabric sweeping the stone paving of the hall. Close. Closer. She turned, raising her arm to ward off the glinting knife in the hand of a hooded creature in a dark robe. She felt a sharp pain as the knife sliced across her fingers and palm, and the blood flowed. She staggered forward. The knife was raised again, and it slashed again, then it plunged through the silk of her sari into her heart. . . .

FRIEND OR FAUX

Joyce Christmas

FAWCETT GOLD MEDAL • NEW YORK

A Fawcett Gold Medal
Published by Ballantine Books
Copyright © 1991 by Joyce Christmas

All rights reserved under International and Pan-American Copyright Conventions. Published in the United States by Ballantine Books, a division of Random House, Inc., New York, and simultaneously in Canada by Random House of Canada Limited, Toronto.

Library of Congress Catalog Card Number: 91-92114

ISBN 0-449-14701-0

Manufactured in the United States of America

First Edition: November 1991

*For Jon Peterson,
with whom I first took
fictional pen in hand*

Chapter 1

*L*ady Margaret Priam was not certain that it had been a good idea to get a fax machine for her home.

The fax in her hand said, "I tried to ring you, but I can't bear your beastly answering machine. There's a problem at the Priory. I need you here at once."

Lady Margaret usually had difficulty deciphering the handwriting of her brother, David, but so far, at least, it was remarkably clear.

Then in a different, highly legible, and possibly feminine hand: "Oh to be in England now that April's here."

As it was already June, the literary allusion suggested to Margaret that the young Earl of Brayfield had attracted yet another young lady with her eye on the possibility of becoming his countess. This one had decided to provide a touch of culture, specifically Browning.

"Ram-Sam has arrived with entourage and intends to stay the summer." This again in David's hand. "The prospect is driving me mad. You could always handle him, and he still likes blondes, so you're the one, unless you've done something purple or green to your hair."

Ram-Sam was now simply Mr. Ramsamai Tharpur, as decreed by the government of India, but in his own mind, to his many of his former subjects, and to some segments of

1

the world, he continued to be His Highness Ramsamai Singh, Maharajah of Tharpur.

Over the years, the maharajah's visits to Margaret's late father at Priam's Priory had invariably sent Margaret's mother to her rooms with a sick headache, but as a child, Margaret had been delighted to accept handfuls of unset diamonds or emeralds from his beautifully manicured, slightly pudgy hand. They were immediately confiscated by her nanny and returned to His Highness in the morning, but yes—Ram-Sam had a particular fondness for blond girls of all ages. And polo, of course. Her father had played a lot of chukkers with His Highness when they were both fit and young and shining lights of what remained of the polo world after World War II.

"You must come at once." David's hand started to decompose. "He must be persuaded to move on. Fax your arrival time. Potts will meet you at Heathrow."

David signed off with a flourish, confident that his sister, older by a half dozen years and therefore wiser when it suited him to think so, would immediately book a flight from New York to England to handle the maharajah.

"No, David," Margaret said aloud. "I will not rush home at your command."

She would simply telephone him now and tell him. It was noon in New York; David and his houseguests would likely be having tea as the English day declined into evening. She picked up the phone in her comfortable East Side Manhattan apartment and dialed the 011 international code. Then she paused.

Her life in New York City had slowed to a near standstill. The antiques shop where she had worked for several years persuading rich society ladies to purchase bits of Chinese jade and porcelain had closed. Although her former employer had arranged a generous severance for services beyond her modest job description, the money would not last forever. She liked to live well, but she was not rich, and she had few qualifications for a high-paying job. The life of an idle, titled English lady making the New York social rounds had never enchanted her, however many free dinners and gala parties were hers for the asking. Even her romantic life was drifting aimlessly, since her most constant companion, Detective Sam De Vere of the New York City police, had disappeared into his work so as to become nearly invisible to her.

True, she was seeing one or two attractive men—who held almost no appeal for her. Not infrequently she wondered if, by arriving at an age slightly past her mid-thirties, she had become too critical of men in general. In any event, none of them came close to comparing favorably with De Vere during happier days.

Margaret made a sudden decision. What was there to keep her in New York? Very little. She dialed the country code to England, and then the familiar number of Priam's Priory off in the peaceful green countryside near the village of Upper Rime.

"Hello? Hello?" A high-pitched, singsong female voice answered. "Hello? Hello? Who are you telephoning, please?"

"Lord Brayfield, please." Margaret was mystified. Where was the butler, Harbert? Or Mrs. Domby, the housekeeper, or even one of the maids?

"Hello? Hello?" The woman said. She sounded like an Indian.

Then: "Blasted woman. Give it here." A sort of muffled giggle and the sound of a scuffle. Finally Harbert's dignified voice came on the line, sounding somewhat harried. "Priam's Priory."

"Harbert? It's Lady Margaret, calling from New York."

"Ahh. So *good* to hear your voice, Lady Margaret." Harbert quickly regained his normal pompous dignity. He had achieved his position as butler and majordomo at Priam's Priory at a fairly young age, only a few years before, coming from some grand country house in the eastern counties to replace the legendary Mr. Noakes of Margaret's childhood. Margaret thus did not know him well, but knew for a certainty that Harbert took his position very seriously. Almost too much so, Margaret thought, given her slightly mad, charming, and unpredictable brother, who took nothing seriously.

"His lordship is out about the estate with . . . with some film people from America," Harbert said.

"No! Not the maharajah *and* a film company." Her brother's occasional business of letting out Priam's Priory for films and television helped pay the expenses, but Harbert sounded as though it was greatly beneath the dignity of the family.

"I understand they are shooting exteriors only," Harbert said grimly, "but the confusion, what with His Highness here, and his wife and the rest of them." He sighed. "One of his . . . his . . . entourage answered the telephone just now. It is a troubling situation." He paused. "Especially with a Second Her Highness in residence." His disapproval came through clearly across the wide Atlantic.

"Do you mean another wife? Ram-Sam brought *two* wives?" Margaret did not think that sort of thing was permitted any longer.

"That is what she is said to be, m'lady, although not . . . a native of His Highness's country."

"Please tell David that I will wind up some affairs here and fly over as soon as I can arrange it."

There was silence, then Harbert said, "Very good, Lady Margaret. I shall have you met if you inform us of your flight."

"Don't trouble," Margaret said. "If I require to be met, I shall let you know, but I will probably find my own way home." She might spend a day or two in London first. David could demand an immediate arrival, but it had never been her position to allow him his way too often. Since childhood, she had used her slight seniority to keep her brother in check, most frequently when he became too demanding on the basis of his status as heir to the lands and titles of the Priam family.

"All this business is stirring up the ghosts," Harbert said gloomily. "One of the maids claims she was accosted by the gray lady. . . ."

"Ah, the ghosts," Margaret said. "In that event, I shall make haste."

* * *

Margaret thought long and hard about whether to try to track down De Vere to tell him she was departing New York, perhaps for an extended period. Then she decided that if his response seemed intended to discourage her from leaving, she would have to deal with a desire to cancel her trip with no assurance that matters between them would change. If he expressed indifference, she would have to deal with the issue of rejection. She was not, she concluded, courageous enough to face either possibility. Instead, around midday, she rang her young friend, Prince Paul Castrocani, at his offices at United National Bank & Trust, far downtown in a sedate corner of financial Manhattan.

She fancied this a crafty move, since Paul shared his Chelsea apartment with De Vere in an amiable arrangement whereby neither was required to pass more than a few hours a month in each other's company. De Vere was dedicated to serving justice via the New York City police department, while Prince Paul was dedicated to finding the perfect young woman, preferably very rich, via any means available. On the other hand, information on Margaret's whereabouts could be passed on by Paul, without the need for Margaret to be personally involved. So much for the vaunted courage of the Priams.

"I seem to be leaving for England late tomorrow," she told Paul when his eager secretary had tracked him down somewhere in the bank, where he had no doubt been puzzling out the meaning of the prime interest rate. Paul was not a notable success as a banker. "There are a few problems at home. Could we meet tonight for dinner?"

"Ah, well . . . yes," Paul said, "certainly. I can arrange something."

"You don't sound taken with the idea," Margaret said. "I may not be back for a long time."

"My mother arrived from Dallas two days ago," he said. "I am scheduled to escort her to some elaborate formal event this evening. Although I have heard that such activities are fewer because money is tight, it seems not the case in my mother's circles. In any event, she enjoys hearing people say that I surely cannot be her son but rather a younger brother. She had hoped to see you on this trip.''

Carolyn Sue Dennis, formerly Princess Castrocani and now Mrs. Benton Hoopes, had some years before rid herself of Paul's father, an impoverished Italian prince, and had gone on to make her mark in her Texas hometown as the very rich wife of the equally rich Ben Hoopes. She appeared sporadically in New York to flaunt her affluence before the city's haute social set. If social New York was beginning to find that overt displays of wealth and self-indulgence no longer played well to the local masses, and if the wealth itself was not what it once was, Carolyn Sue was never bothered by such concerns. Not now, not ever.

''Unless you and she can dine with me tonight, I must miss her,'' Margaret said.

''She certainly cannot,'' Paul said. ''I believe the requirements of preparing herself to go on display will prevent it. There is a ballet performance first that I have already declined to attend. You and I might have an early dinner, and I will join her in time to whisk her around the dance floor.''

''Lovely,'' Margaret said. ''I need to set my mind straight about returning to England, and seeing to some silly business about an old maharajah who was a friend of my father's and who has moved into the family home for an extended stay.''

''I see,'' Paul said. ''And obviously you wish to impress me with the desirability of informing De Vere of your whereabouts, should he inquire.''

''Certainly not! I haven't even spoken to him in ages.''

''I see,'' Paul said. ''It will do you no good to ask me what he has been doing. I know nothing.''

Margaret booked her flight and winced at the cost, began tidying up her affairs for an open-ended return to her homeland, and berated herself silently for choosing to leave De Vere behind without a personal word.

Meanwhile, her brother, David Priam, the twenty-second Earl of Brayfield, led a motley crew of dinner guests into the formal dining room at Priam's Priory. The candles had been lit and the heavy old silver had been polished to a glow by Harbert. The linen was snowy white and thick, and masses of flowers from the Priory's gardens filled the priceless Georgian silver epergne at the center of the long table. Ancestral portraits in gilded frames hung on the cream-colored walls above the crystal decanters on the mahogany sideboard.

Mrs. Domby in her role as cook to the household had provided a nice plate of cold asparagus to start and a lovely roast chicken, with a blackberry ice to finish. But, as she said at least three times to Harbert, what with Indian princes sitting down with rich Americans and those film people and his lordship, there was no telling who would be pleased. And with food being consumed at a great rate, someone would have to be off to London again soon to restock the larder. Harrods would deliver, of course, but on its own schedule, and there were always items forgotten until the last minute, too late to telephone to London.

The young earl found the necessity of entertaining his incompatible guests tiresome, but in one way or another, they represented the promise of many pounds paid in return for goods and services, enough to keep the old Priory going for the rest of the year, if all went well. He lounged at the head of his table, and longed for a quick release to his private rooms.

The Maharajah of Tharpur, portly and elegant and splendidly jacketed in brocade that harked back to the glory days of the Indian princes, was seated beside Miss Jazmin Burns, the platinum-tressed gift of Hollywood films to the world. On his left was Miss Chloe Waters of Figge Hall, Warwickshire, and Sloane Street, London. She could recite patches of both Browning and Tennyson, and even some bits of Keats. She quoted no immortal lines tonight, however, preferring to pout at being placed some distance from David.

Quintus Roach, also of Hollywood, found himself next to Mrs. Lester Flood (Phyllis to her friends), late of someplace in the middle of America and only recently a new neighbor of the earl. The empty chair on Roach's other side was soon taken by the young Englishwoman who styled herself the second wife of the maharajah. She had delayed her appearance to make a dramatic entrance in silken sari threaded with gold and an excess of gem-encrusted baubles. She swept through doors held open for her by the butler. Roach, who had spent too many years in Hollywood not succeeding in show business, was unimpressed.

Lester Flood, was pleased that he had been seated on the other side of the luscious Jazmin Burns, who was momentarily displeased at being upstaged by an upstart maharani who had chosen to don the national dress of a country of which she was obviously not a native. He did not really believe that he had heard Jazmin murmur, "Ah, the English bitch of life."

Across the table from Lester was a rather seedy Priam cousin, to whom Lester had lost quite a bit of money at a London gambling club a few months before. Nigel Priam had dropped by unexpectedly, as the party enjoyed preprandial drinks in the immense Tudor Great Hall, and had accepted the earl's reluctant invitation to dine. He had not changed for dinner. Lester himself wore black tie, and had to admit that his new Savile Row tailor had done a fine job of making him look much trimmer than he actually was. And Lester thought Phyllis looked just fine in one of those designer dresses she'd bought in Paris, although since her facelift, she often had some difficulty in forming her mouth into a smile.

Mrs. Domby peered in from the pantry, and noted that no one had much conversation except the incessant Mr. Roach, who was regaling the table with tales of devious Hollywood agents, corrupt producers, and sex-crazed starlets, none of whom were known to the assembled party. A flurry of interest ensued at the mention of Sylvester Stallone and Clint Eastwood, but subsided as soon as it was clear that Roach knew neither of them personally.

"His Highness's wife indeed, Mr. Harbert," Mrs. Domby whispered over her shoulder as she took in the new maharani fitting a cigarette into a very long, jeweled holder. "The old countess would never have permitted this wife business. And certainly no one smoked during dinner." Mrs. Domby's outrage got no response from Harbert except a frown. He took himself off to pour more wine. "They won't be sitting about late," she said aloud to her empty kitchen. "Eat and be off, mark my words."

The dinner hour ended quickly, as Mrs. Domby had predicted. Before she had finished up in the kitchen, with Tilda, the maid on late duty, to help out, the guests had scattered, minutes after the men had finished their port and joined the ladies for coffee in the drawing room.

"The standards are going down, Mr. Harbert," Mrs. Domby began, but Harbert was already locking up the wine cabinet.

"I don't have time for idle talk about our guests," he said sternly. "I have business to attend to. This house is a great responsibility." He soon departed, leaving her the key to the silver chest in the pantry. Relations had never been warm between them, but Mrs. Domby was beginning to think that Harbert was getting above himself.

Mrs. Domby looked out the windows of her kitchen. It was almost dark, and she heard the patter of raindrops on the pebbled drive, the first June shower they'd had in days. She switched off the lights and made her way to the back stairs.

The house was almost in darkness, with only a night light glowing in the long hallway that ran parallel to the Great Hall. She stopped and listened. It seemed to her that behind the sound of the rain, she heard voices coming from the Great Hall. She peered down the hallway, and thought she glimpsed one of the Indian ladies wearing that sari thing they wrapped around themselves instead of a decent dress.

Mrs. Domby shook her head. She had had quite enough of these foreigners from the East and America all in one dose.

As she started up the stairs that would take her to her comfy room on the top floor (his lordship had given her a lovely new color telly in honor of her thirty years of service), she heard the unmistakable sound of Jazmin Burns's merry false laugh, and a hearty chuckle that she was sure was His Highness.

Such goings-on would never have been permitted when the present earl's mother was alive.

Mrs. Domby made her way to her bed, and the drumming rain blotted out any further sounds that might have raised in or about the ancient house.

Chapter 2

The heavy embroidered sari worn by Her Highness Laxmi, the recognized Maharani of Tharpur for some forty years, fluttered behind her as she padded quietly along a dark hallway in Priam's Priory. It was after eleven by the Priory's clocks. The house was still, but she knew she must find her husband sitting late with the young earl in a room at the end of this corridor, which the silly English maids called the Nun's Walk. And with him would be the monstrous woman who claimed to be Second Her Highness, but who was nothing more than a stupid sow of an Englishwoman named Doris whom the maharajah pretended to have married three years ago. An ugly, awkward blonde with feet too big and limbs too pink, who would never wear a sari gracefully. Her Highness's sleek, still black hair was covered with a filmy silk shawl, and the bangles on her arms clicked softly. She wore little other jewelry except for a favorite necklace of small diamonds set in gold filigree—but then, she no longer traveled with her good jewelry as she had when her husband was still a ruling prince. As she moved, she kept her back straight and held her head high, as a woman of royal lineage should.

Her Highness stopped in the damp, musty passageway and listened. Her eyes were not good nowadays, and spectacles were not dignified, but her hearing was sharp. She looked back down the long hall. The housekeeper had said that few people ventured into this old hallway after dark, so she had chosen her circuitous route to elude the maharajah's enemies, who spoke in whispers of lies and treachery. Her heart began to pound, although she was certain no one had seen her enter the passageway through the outside door near the kitchen.

The rain had caught her unaware as she crept out of the house on a devious path to her goal, and she had only barely managed to keep out of the downpour before reaching shelter. This old house with its sudden stairs and odd passageways leading to unexpected rooms and curious dead ends reminded her of the old Tharpur palaces in India where she had spent her life. Although she kept aloof from the inhabitants of Priam's Priory, she had learned her way about, and this now stood her in good stead as she went forth on her critical errand.

Her Highness Laxmi had been the maharajah's wife since she was twelve years old, and he himself had been a mere boy of seventeen and heir to the throne of the small but rich princely state of Tharpur. The great war of the British against the Germans and Japanese was ending, and the old maharajah, his grandfather, was dying of an excess of good living. It had not been the grandest wedding in history, but the elephants had worn their old golden ornaments, and the attending rajahs and highnesses had donned their best jewels. The maharani shook her head to push away those memories. The past was over. These were new times, more difficult times, and it was her duty to protect her husband, even if they rarely spoke now. She had even agreed to accompany him to England, which she found damp and cold no matter what the season. She longed for the dry, intense heat of Tharpur, and the shadowy, cool chambers of the old summer palace in the middle of the lake, the desolate reddish plains and hills, and the village women in their bright green and yellow and red saris, the camels pulling their rickety, overloaded two-wheel carts. They would go back soon, when she had told the maharajah what she had overheard of the plots and wickedness that surrounded them in this horrible place.

Much as she shrank from the public scene that lay ahead, she would do her duty as a proper Indian wife. Not like this greedy, treacherous Doris—Devi, she called herself now—who did not know how to behave, and who hated everything about India. Doris could stay behind in England when they left. She *would* stay behind, of that Her Highness was certain.

The maharani peered again into the darkness. She thought she saw a dark shadow move across the passage, but it might have been a trick of her weak eyes. She did not believe the stories of these pale English ghosts the maids had been speaking of. The ladies who served her were far more sensible. She moved forward, intent on reaching the dark-paneled sitting room with its strange white columns at the end of the passageway.

She heard the rustle of fabric sweeping the stone paving of the hall. Close. Closer. She turned, raising her arm to ward off the glinting knife in the hand of a hooded creature in a dark robe. She felt a sharp pain as the knife sliced across her fingers and palm, and the blood flowed. She staggered forward. The knife was raised again, and it slashed again, then it plunged through the silk of her sari into her heart.

The old Maharani of Tharpur fell back onto the hard stone floor. As her life slipped away, she managed to turn and stretch out her bloody hand, to imprint the pale gray stone with one, two, three red handprints. She did not feel the diamond necklace being ripped from her throat, or hear the footsteps hurry back the way they had come.

When Her Highness Laxmi, Maharani of Tharpur, died in the ghost-ridden, ancient hallway of Priam's Priory, Margaret and Paul were eating osso buco and discussing De Vere in a roundabout way.

"He has always been a private person," Paul said. "I think I do not know him at all. I understand that he does not entirely approve of me, although I believe he likes me. I am certain that he likes you, but to what degree, I cannot say."

"You men always stick together."

Paul laughed. "Truly, Margaret, I have no sense at all of what he thinks and feels. Yes, I will inform him of your departure. Beyond that, I promise nothing. He would be more likely to listen to my mother. He quite admires her grand disregard for anything that money can't buy.''

''But Carolyn Sue has money to buy anything.''

''So you see,'' Paul said, ''she therefore has a great regard for everything. I wish I were so rich, rather than a son kept in near poverty. I am a prince, after all.''

Margaret chuckled. ''Carolyn Sue is very generous to you. And it isn't always good to be very rich and a prince, because it's terribly hard to adjust if you are suddenly a poor one. This old maharajah I'm going to see used to be unbelievably rich, but hard times have come for the Indian princes.'' Then she thought a moment. ''But old Ram-Sam was probably clever enough to remove the Tharpur riches safely abroad years ago. Paul, you cannot imagine the way the highnesses lived even back when I was a child and the best days were over. They had the most fabulous jewels, cars by the dozens, trunks full of gorgeous clothes, alligator cases, solid gold this, diamond-encrusted that—the best of everything. Ram-Sam turned Priam's Priory on its head when he came to us. His wife came once, a rather retiring, old-fashioned woman, very religious, but kind to us children. The maharajah, on the other hand, was quite the man of the world. And didn't David and I love to creep about to catch glimpses of this exotic creature in our midst. Even when we were small, we heard of the little scandals about the dancing girls and actresses he was involved with. At least he spared my poor mother the necessity of dealing with a second wife. That has been reserved for my dear brother.''

''Ahhh.'' Paul's interest was piqued. ''He has more than one wife?''

''Apparently Highness recently acquired another one, although I doubt if it's a strictly legal business. But our butler indicated that Ram-Sam has brought along a woman who styles herself Second Her Highness.''

Paul was thoughtful. ''I wonder if having multiple wives would solve my problem. One very, very rich—perhaps even old and ugly—the other very, very young and beautiful. . . . ''

"Paul! It is definitely not allowed for the likes of you. And I do think having more than one wife offers more problems than advantages," Margaret said, not knowing that for the Maharajah of Tharpur, the problems created by multiple wives, even if one was a faux bride of the East, had been resolved.

"Very nasty business," the village constable of Upper Rime said aloud to himself. He was alone in a long hallway at Priam's Priory, except for the body of the maharani, which had been discovered by a shrieking housemaid as she went about her early morning tasks. He knew that the hall was a remnant of the twelfth-century priory that had once stood on these lands and sheltered monks and nuns before old Henry VIII snatched it away and handed it over to the Priams. The constable was not superstitious, but he was not comfortable in the old hallway. He had heard the stories of the ghosts since he was a lad. However, since he was both ambitious and bright, it was immediately clear to him that the murder of the wife (*one* of the wives!) of an Indian prince (former prince, but the glamour still clung to him), and a very rich one to boot if you trusted the village gossip, was more than he wished to handle on his own for even a quarter hour. Add to that the scene of the crime being the home of the earl, and there was more than just a spot of trouble afoot. Not that the constable held David Priam in especially high regard; he thought him a pokey-nosed lad who had nothing much to recommend him but his title and this old house and all the lands around it.

The constable wasted no time in finding a more senior policeman to take charge.

"Very nasty business," a senior but still local policeman said to the Earl of Brayfield, who received him formally in the Great Hall under imposing dark rafters and a soaring roof. "I've been hearing rumors all around about the gold and jewels these highnesses brought with them. It'll be in the London papers soon enough, mark my words. The press has already been spotted in the village. A couple of coves on motorbikes have been asking questions.''

''I hope not,'' David said. He was tall and fair, and often seemed to dwell in a state of abstraction. Many young ladies found him exceedingly attractive, but whether it was his person or his lineage that aroused their interest, it was not easy to tell. The fact that he was still unmarried at thirty with a string of broken hearts behind him only added to his appeal. He appeared to find murder in his large country house an irritation rather than a matter of deep distress.

''I don't like this sort of business,'' the policeman said doggedly, in an attempt to elicit some sort of concentrated response from the earl. David Priam, however, stood before the huge carved fireplace with his hands behind his back and gazed fixedly at a large portrait that might have been the first Queen Elizabeth, painted in the style of Holbein.

''We've done our pictures,'' the policeman continued, ''and all the crime scene business. The medical man suggests that a necklace or the like was torn from her neck, so we'll look into that carefully. It could have been a break-in with an eye to robbing the place, but you never know.''

''I believe my staff is careful about locking up,'' David said, ''although nowadays the determined criminal can get around any sort of security barriers. I hope matters are cleared quickly. I hate having my houseguests inconvenienced.''

The policeman hesitated. ''The . . . um . . . maharajah doesn't have what you could call ruling person status any longer, but I understand he is well known in very high quarters.''

''Polo,'' David said absently. ''He no longer plays, but from time to time in recent years, he has umpired at Windsor.''

''Ah, very high circles indeed.'' The policeman appeared to be picturing the Maharajah of Tharpur chatting up the Prince and Princess of Wales at the polo matches at Windsor

Great Park. "I've called in someone senior to assist. Someone from Scotland Yard is due very soon," he said.

"Not to mention my sister," David said. "This is going to make her very cross."

Chapter 3

Margaret telephoned Priam's Priory as soon as she had collected her luggage at Heathrow Airport, so as to reassure David that help was on the way, eventually. She had decided to spend the next two days in London, and have Potts fetch her at Claridge's to drive the hour and a half into the country-side and home.

Harbert came on the line in a state that might be termed, for him, unnerved. He conducted a monologue: A body in the Nun's Walk. David with the police. The maharajah incommunicado. The Priory in an uproar. Film people treading on the ancient lawns.

"A body?" Margaret chose the most striking of the star-tling options presented by Harbert. He had apparently es-chewed the Speak, Listen, Respond sequence of a normal telephone conversation. "Please do be calm," she added.

"I am entirely calm, m'lady," he said. "It was one of His Highness's ladies. The old maharani. The true wife."

"Good gracious," Margaret said. "A heart attack? An accident?"

"They say it was murder," Harbert said.

Margaret felt a rush of distress. "Surely not," she said.

"She was stabbed in the Nun's Walk," Harbert said. "There can be no mistake of that." Then he added, "The

18

Indian party has a tendency to take liberties with the house and find themselves where they don't belong.''

"Harbert," Margaret said firmly, "I shall hire a car here at the airport and drive directly to the Priory." She had misgivings about the state of morning traffic on the M25 and then the M40 toward Oxford, but there seemed no other choice. "Do they have the murderer in hand?"

"The perpetrator is unknown," Harbert said. "The police say an intruder." He paused. "The staff is saying that it was one of the ghosts. The nun, because of the scene of the crime."

"Nonsense," Margaret said. "The nun is entirely benevolent. The gray lady, on the other hand, seems to enjoy terrorizing those who encounter her. But she has never been seen in the Nun's Walk." Then she realized that she was seriously discussing the possibility that one of the Priory's two ghosts had done a murder. "Harbert, ghosts might frighten one to death, but they do not wield knives. Please remind the staff of this."

"I shall do so," Harbert said. He was not amused. "And I will inform your brother of your impending arrival."

Tiresome man, she thought.

The accumulated weariness of an overnight flight from New York and the torturous drive from the airport dropped away as Margaret neared the narrow road leading to the village of Upper Rime. The village had not much changed in the few years since she was last home. The brick- and limestone-fronted buildings dressed up with potted geraniums and climbing roses still pressed close to the narrow pavements. No Golden Arches had yet found their way to Upper Rime. The cricket pitch on the village green, with its clumps of sheltering trees on the perimeter, awaited the weekend matches. A large sign at the end of the green proclaimed the semiannual village fair—this year featuring Wilson's Steam Fair with stupendous rides and challenging games for the entire family. Workmen were already unloading bright red and gold stands from lorries, and assembling a spanking bright merry-go-round with prancing white horses and gilded reins.

As a child, Margaret had looked forward to the June fair with tense excitement. Would she toss the ring far enough to win a garish but much-desired stuffed animal? Would her disapproving nanny allow her a second ride on the wildly decorated merry-go-round on a wooden steed so much more romantic than her own placid white pony?

One or two older village ladies on their way to do their marketing recognized Margaret and waved. Home again, she thought. Then she remembered what lay ahead. Everyone in the village would be whispering behind lace curtains and wooden shutters, at the greengrocer's and at the butcher's shop, about the murder at Priam's Priory. Speculation about the event would be intense in the dark corners of the Riming Man Pub, which looked to be doing a lively business even this early.

Beyond the village lay the narrow road with high hedge-rows on either side that would bring her to the gates of the Priory. The countryside was green, dotted with clusters of yellow and white wildflowers, and the trees were heavy with new June leaves. For the moment, at least, the sun shone and there were no ominous distant clouds to threaten afternoon rain.

Margaret caught her breath and swerved to avoid the on-coming rush of a huge motorbike ridden by a resolutely black-leather-clad person. It appeared that some of the noisier and more perilous aspects of modern life had come to Upper Rime after all.

When she reached the top of a small hill and could see over the hedgerows, she looked across the meadows toward the old manor house, part of the Priam holdings but uninhabited for years. The front was masked in scaffolding, and several workmen were seen attempting to repair the ravages of centuries. Margaret sighed. Her brother certainly couldn't afford to restore the old manor, but in his constant search for funds to maintain the Priory, he must have made good his intention to sell it off to an unsuspecting lover of history and/or dry rot. Good luck to the new owner.

Now she passed the stubby stone pillars that guarded the drive to the house. The faint outline of three crenellated Priam towers carved into the gray stone was still visible. The sandy drive was lined with a double row of slim poplars, and beyond them, stands of ancient oaks on the one side, and on the other, cultivated fields and pastures where a cluster of black and white cows grazed. She never failed to experience a homecoming thrill of the sight of the charming, irregular chimneys of Priam's Priory on her right hand, rising above the trees.

The single discordant note: two huge shiny white caravans parked in a field. No doubt they housed the film people David had mentioned. Away to her left, a stream meandered toward a placid lake, with a crumbling eighteenth-century marble rotunda, like a little classical temple, poised over the water. A thin plume of smoke rose up into the blue summer sky.

A morning such as this, even with a murder just up the drive, made her wonder why she had ever chosen to exchange it for the clangorous rigors of Manhattan.

She drove through the arched stone gatehouse, past the low, ivy-covered wall around the house, and came to a stop in the pebbled courtyard. She sat for a moment cherishing the sight of the rosy bricks, the majestic windows, the odd gables, and the tall chimneys. Not a perfectly symmetrical house like some of the grand country houses she knew, but it had an endearing crooked charm, and it was home.

The film people had made inroads in the courtyard. Monstrous lights on high stands with trailing cables snaking across the gravel had been placed at a corner of the drive. A youngish man with a beard was fiddling with what looked like a portable movie camera, while an older man was fitting together a set of wooden rail tracks. More interesting to Margaret was a serious-looking black car parked in front of the entrance. It carried the aura of officialdom, and it could only signify that the police were within. A pity it was no longer possible to identify a London car by its plates, but Margaret would not be surprised to find that Scotland Yard was on the case. For a brief moment she thought it was quite like stepping into a classic detective novel, but immediately reminded herself that the situation she was entering was not at all cozy and Miss Marple-ish.

Before she let herself into the house, she took another long look at the familiar facade.

"Oy, miss. You can't park there." A plump, rosy-cheeked man in well-worn work clothes appeared from around the corner of the house. It was old Potts, who had been fetching, carrying, and tidying up for as long as Margaret could remember. "And if you're the press, you can move right along. You've got no business here."

"Good day to you, Potts. Here are the keys. Park it where it suits you. And please ask someone to bring in my cases."

"Ah, Lady Margaret. I didn't make you out. A welcome sight you are, if I may say so."

"As are you," she said. "The house is looking fine, too."

"Well, m'lady, it's still ours, and that's something. Not yet belonging to the National Trust with day-trippers tramping through all summer long. We still get the historians who want a glimpse of the bits of the old priory building, and the Great Hall."

"And the ghost hunters?"

"Still come begging to look about, with their cameras and the electrical machines to test for the spirits."

Margaret laughed. "And neither ghost wants anything to do with them."

"True enough," Potts said. "They only walk when . . ." He stopped and shook his head. "When there's trouble, or so it seems. You'll have had the news from his lordship."

"I have had a brief summary of events from Harbert," Margaret said, "but my opinion is that ghosts do not do murder."

"I pray not," Potts said. "But I'm glad I go home to the village and my good wife every night. Here now, let me see to the car and the cases, and you go right in. Door's unlatched."

It pleased Margaret that David continued to struggle to keep the house private, the farms profitable, and most of the grounds kept up. He'd once had a scheme to make the house into a hotel—or rather a grand retreat for a few high-paying guests. Then he had considered a conference center, where study groups or businessmen from abroad could pursue their concerns undistracted, and still be a convenient distance from London.

The sale of the decrepit manor house would help finances, and David had once contemplated selling off the old polo field her father had maintained until his death for country weekend homes for affluent Londoners. The villagers, however, were probably not keen on seeing the earl bring in hordes of city people.

As she mounted the stone steps to the heavy oak door, she wondered if her father's ancient polo ponies still lived on in their old stables, although they must be close to twenty years old. Certainly there was no one to keep them in training, as David had not inherited the late earl's love of the sport. David kept only a couple of hunters to be prepared to ride with the local hunt, and cut a swathe through the young sporting women of the county.

Margaret took a deep breath and pushed open the door.

Before her on the wall hung the early-seventeenth-century portrait of the first earl, who was remarkably like David. The doors to the three-story Great Hall—the only true relic of Elizabethan days—were closed. The house was very quiet. David and the police would be conferring in the library or the morning room, which overlooked the lawns on the other side of the house.

Margaret heard a snuffle and a low "woof." She peered down the long hallway that ran parallel to the Great Hall, and saw an ancient black retriever blundering heavily along the passage toward her.

"Wally? Is it Wally?"

The dog raised its graying muzzle and looked at her through aged eyes. A feeble wag of his tail signified that he had recognized his name, and indeed the voice of the speaker herself. He proceeded slowly along the stone-paved corridor with its scattering of faded oriental rugs and cabinets crammed with historic Priam objects, and finally sniffed her outstretched hand.

"Dear Wally, I haven't been away so long that you have

forgotten me, have you?'' The tail wagged again, vigorously. He knew her well. "Where is everyone?"

Wally had no suggestions. He simply sat at Margaret's feet and leaned against her legs.

"Lovely boy," she said, and ruffled his soft, floppy ears.

"So, what's going on here?" The American voice startled Margaret.

A man in a handsome tweed jacket with artful leather elbow patches, worn over a black turtleneck, emerged from the Great Hall. He was wearing jodhpurs, and carrying— Margaret had to look again—a riding crop.

"I beg your pardon," Margaret said, "but what *is* going on here?" Wally got to his feet and ambled over to the man. A tentative wag of his tail indicated familiarity, if not cordiality.

"Murder," the man said, "and I don't like it one bit." He peered at her. "Don't I know you from somewhere?"

"Yes," Margaret said. She had indeed met him once in California, at a spectacular house in the Hollywood Hills. His name was Quintus Roach, and he was not a very successful film producer and director.

"I got it! Marvin Smith's place, out in California." Quintus Roach seemed delighted.

"Correct," Margaret said. "And you are planning to do some expensive filming here."

He looked at her sharply. "If this murder doesn't screw it up," he said. "The police are delaying us some. You heard about the murder?"

"A bit," Margaret said.

"It's a real mess," Quintus Roach said. "This guy used to be a maharajah, see? Like in those old movies we saw as kids. So he turns up here with a couple of wives, which is not such a bad idea when you think about it. Anyway, the older wife is stabbed to death night before last. The cops are saying publicly it was robbery, some guy was out to steal her jewelry. Now, a smart thief would have taken a good look around a place like this and stolen something worthwhile, not a handful of cheap diamonds. I mean, you ought to see what the other wife was wearing." Margaret detected a faint leer. Roach was not finished. "If you ask me, there are plenty of people closer at hand that I'd point a finger at instead of some robber. Listen." He lowered his voice. "I told the cop, the constable, that I saw this dead Indian lady poking her nose into other people's business, listening at doors. I'd come around a corner, and there she'd be, just scooting through a door. That kinda annoys people, you know? He just wrote it down in his little black book. But what do these people know?"

"I don't really know what these people know," Margaret said, "but I do wonder where my brother is."

"Brother?"

"David Priam. The householder. The Earl of Brayfield," Margaret said hopefully.

"Geez. You mean that kid the earl is your brother? Whaddaya know? Small world."

"Yes," Margaret said. "Almost too small."

Chapter 4

*M*argaret *was* saved from further conversation with Quintus Roach by the breathless arrival of Mrs. Domby. At a stern look from her, Roach retreated hastily into the Great Hall.

"Mr. Harbert said you'd be here in good time, Lady Margaret, and here you are. Don't you look pretty and fit?" Mrs. Domby was an ample and firmly corseted servant of the old school, who had started out as a maid and had risen to become housekeeper and cook in one, now that the number of residents at the Priory had been reduced to her brother and his occasional houseguests. For as long as Margaret could remember, she had fancied a virulent henna rinse for her hair. Margaret and her mother used to speculate that it was some outward manifestation of a frustrated femme fatale lurking beneath the otherwise proper exterior.

Mrs. Domby looked Margaret over. "It doesn't appear all that nasty American pollution and those drug addicts that attack you as you go about your business have done you any harm." Mrs. Domby had a taste for American television programs, the seamier the better. "Not that things don't happen here, oh, yes they do. Terrible things. *Murder* in this house. Shocking. There hasn't been such a thing since that trollop was murdered by her husband and decided to haunt us." Mrs. Domby referred to a tragic death some two cen-

26

turies ago, but the river of time flowed through Priam's Priory at an extremely slow pace, so it was viewed as recent history. "Of course," Mrs. Domby added with disapproval, "with these foreigners settled in, you expect the worst."

Like most of the older servants, Mrs. Domby herself had once been a "foreigner," who had come from another part of England to work at the Priory. Margaret's mother and grandmother before her believed the local people gossiped too much about the family, and only hired outsiders. Until she died, Margaret's mother even retained the quaint notion that unmarried servants were more reliable. Nowadays, things were different. Although Mrs. Domby's title signified her seniority rather than her marital status, Potts had long ago acquired a wife, and the maids and outside men were mostly local folk. Harbert had come from elsewhere, but that likely would have been a career move, a step up from serving a baronet to running the home of an earl.

"You're looking very well yourself," Margaret said, choosing to ignore her commentary, but Mrs. Domby was not quite finished.

"Americans. The ones who bought the manor are . . ." She sniffed in a way that Margaret interpreted to mean, "Not our kind, but we'll see." Mrs. Domby shook her head. "The Roach man you were talking to is a shabby specimen. And that woman he has with him . . ."

"He's staying here with a woman?"

"I wouldn't say 'with' in the usual sense," Mrs. Domby said. "She's an American film star, having something to do with this business with Mr. Roach. Jazmin Burns, she calls herself. She insisted on the Queen's Bedroom, wouldn't you know? I didn't tell her how uncomfortable that bed is, but she hasn't complained yet."

"I know of her," Margaret said. Jazmin Burns was a conspicuous manifestation of the drive to fame and fortune via heavy coverage by the American media. She was a favorite of "Entertainment Tonight" and *The National Enquirer*, but her acting ability was not confirmed by any review of her films that Margaret had read. Her lavish, blond, voluptuous looks did not seem entirely suited to anything that might be filmed with Priam's Priory as a setting.

"Now, I don't mind His Highness," Mrs. Domby said. "We've had the dear maharajah coming to stay for years. Polite as can be, and *most* generous, although the ladies he brought this time are a bit of a trial. I don't know what you'd call 'em, servants of some sort. I had to stop them from cooking *upstairs* in their wing, so they brought all those smelly things down into *my* kitchen. Well, I put a stop to that. One and one only, I said, or go build your fires outdoors. Your uncle Mr. Lawrence likes the concoctions they make. . . . "

"I ought to see David right away," Margaret said quickly. Mrs. Domby's garrulous familiarity was one of the inconveniences of Priam's Priory, along with uncomfortable antique beds of historical significance.

"He's off among the arches," Mrs. Domby said, in reference to the old room that had once been part of the priory's undercroft, and still retained part of the barrel-vaulted ceiling. The canons of the old priory used this as their chapter house. The historians said it had been a double priory, with nuns as well, but they had lived apart in allegedly (and to Margaret's mind, unfairly) far more austere surroundings, now vanished but for the connecting cloister that had been designated the Nun's Walk. The undercroft had been mostly a ruin during Margaret's childhood, but when David came into his inheritance, he had fashioned it into a comfortable personal retreat, so he could avoid the more formal library and sitting room if he chose.

"I'll find him," Margaret said.

"I'll see that your cases are taken up to your room. Tilda will unpack, although I can't vouch for her state of mind. She found the body, you know."

"I see. I don't suppose you have any ideas. . . . "

Mrs. Domby pursed her lips. "Plenty of ideas, Lady Margaret, but it wouldn't be seemly to gossip." She paused, and proceeded to gossip. "Two wives His Highness brought, can you imagine it? That's trouble right there." She sniffed her disapproval. No decent man she knew of would have more than one wife at a time. "To think that an English girl would—"

"I'll just go off and find David," Margaret said hastily, "and see what he knows of this affair." She started down the long corridor toward the other side of the house, with Wally lumbering behind her.

"He's with the man from Scotland Yard," Mrs. Domby said to her back. "Not much to recommend him, if you ask me. Hasn't done a bit of detecting as far as I can tell. But don't you worry. Since the murder, I go around after Mr. Harbert at night to be sure we're all locked in safe."

But Margaret was already well down the hall, into her childhood. Here she had run races, ridden her bicycle, spilled her tea, and tracked in mud. Here she had glided gracefully (she hoped) in her first grown-up ball gown, and here she had walked hand in hand with the young man to whom she had been married for a brief and ultimately unhappy time.

At the end of the corridor, an open door showed a glimpse of the venerable lawns with the broad stripes left by the huge cylinder mower that Potts loved to ride as he cut the grass. The lawns stretched toward the gnarled oaks that had probably sheltered the monks at their prayers, and the few trees that had survived the Dutch elm disease. She could smell the newly cut grass, and she longed to pause to savor the summer's day. Instead she turned right along the screen's passage behind the wall of the Great Hall, then through the formal dining room, and out a low door, down three white stone steps, and into the twelfth century.

David's sitting room was divided into three bays by a row of white stone columns with simple, elegant vaulting forming the roof. A row of windows—fairly modern but with a medieval feel—were open to let in the light and the scents of June from the lush walled garden now at its peak with a riot of red, blue, white, and yellow flowers and the hum of honeybees. Forming one side of the garden was the cloisterlike Nun's Walk, where First Her Highness had met her unexpected end.

"I am here," Margaret said, "as requested."

David gazed up at Margaret thoughtfully from his deep, comfortable armchair. At his side was that essential element of modern life, his fax machine. A mild-looking middle-aged man in the chair opposite stood up. After a moment, David stood as well and came to her. He kissed Margaret on each cheek casually, as though it had been merely weeks instead of nearly two years since he had seen her.

"It is my sister, from New York," David said. "Margaret, this is Inspector Westron, up from London. He's here about the maharajah's wife. She died unexpectedly a day or two ago."

"I heard it was murder," Margaret said. "How d'you do, Inspector. You are here to solve it."

"Mmm. I was sent round at the request of the local people." He had a round, expressionless face, and wore a correct dark gray suit, more like a foreign service person than a policeman. "Mr. Tharpur seems to have lofty connections, and we wanted to keep it all as civilized as possible."

"Murder isn't terribly civilized, is it?" Margaret said. "Poor woman. I met her as a child when she visited with His Highness, who was playing polo with my father. I saw a bit of her when I went out to India to visit Tharpur. I can't imagine her as a victim of murder."

"To tell the truth, we are not viewing it as a personal crime against the woman. The local people are very efficient, and have found some evidence that someone broke in to rob. . . . " Westron did not seem entirely comfortable with this explanation, but no doubt he was obliged to express the official view.

Margaret sighed inwardly. She had come up against the convenient excuse of a random intruder breaking in where no break-in had ever occurred before. Indeed, inadvertently coming upon a murder or two over the past couple of years, she had learned to understand that people didn't like to suspect someone they actually knew of committing murder. The random intruder was so much more, well, *civilized*, even given the state of modern civilization.

"I can't imagine why Mrs. Tharpur Number One decided

to wander down the Nun's Walk in the middle of the night,"
David said. "None of the staff likes it after dark because of
the ghost. And in any case, the Indian camp is located in the
wing on the opposite side of the house. They've rather taken
over and upset the arrangements I've made with this Hollywood fellow to film some bits at the Priory." He sounded
put out. "Of course, she might have been looking for us after
dinner," he added, "and gotten lost."

"Us," Westron said. "I wanted to ask again about you
and your guests."

"As I stated to the constable and the local inspector, I had
some people to dine," David said. "The maharajah and his
lady—his other wife, that is to say." Westron raised a faintly
shocked eyebrow as David continued. "Mr. Roach, the man
from Hollywood, and Jazmin Burns, the American film star.
They're both staying at the Priory while they shoot scenes
about the grounds. A friend, Chloe Waters, is up from London. My cousin Nigel Priam stopped by and joined us."

Margaret blinked at the name of their ne'er-do-well cousin.
"Nigel?"

"He went off blessedly early. Bound for London, he said."
David had never gotten on with Nigel. "And I had these
Americans who . . ." He hesitated. "I've sold them Rime
Manor, did I tell you?"

"No," Margaret said. "You did not, but I have heard."

"Phyllis and Lester Flood," he said, aiming at an American accent. "Right fine folks. We'll discuss it later."

Phyllis and Lester Flood were names Margaret had heard
spoken of—not always kindly—in certain New York circles:
obscenely rich but socially unfinished outsiders from the
Midwest who had tried to make a dent in Manhattan society
by dint of shedding money like leaves for charity and the
arts. Their dollars were accepted; they were not. Apparently
unaffected by matters like economic downturns and international political turbulence, they seemed to have moved on
to conquer different worlds, starting with a rotting manor
house in Upper Rime.

"It was a sufficiently disharmonious group that we didn't
sit about late after we'd dined, so no one knows a thing

about Her Highness,'' David said. "In fact, I'd say no-body outside of me and the servants ever laid eyes on her."

The Yard man said, "I've heard the rumors from the local people that the so-called maharajah had a fortune in jewels with him. He denies that absolutely, via the surviving . . . um . . . Tharpur lady." He was being careful. "We haven't been allowed to interview him. His late wife supposedly had a few pieces with her. The diamond necklace she was said to have been wearing has disappeared, but from all reports, it was not an especially valuable piece, certainly nothing like a royal treasure. Still, someone might have thought to take a dangerous chance, and it ended up with an unintended death."

"This is all such a bother," David said. "I have no idea what Ram-Sam brought with him. He had a vanload of trunks that could have been filled with jewels or a lot of tourist trinkets." He ran his fingers through his longish hair, and sighed deeply.

"You are being rather calm about this, David," she said.

"I assure you, Ram-Sam is supplying all the emotion that is necessary," David said. "I managed a few words with him through a closed door. He seems distressed by his wife's murder, although he's quite smitten with the newest addition to his entourage. At least he was when he arrived. Then Jazmin turned up." David sat down and frowned.

Westron spoke up. "I have information, again via this . . . other wife, that the maharajah believes he is being persecuted by his own government. We are naturally reluctant to believe that his government resorts to assassination, but he insists that the maharani was the first victim of this plot against him, and he is the next." Westron cleared his throat discreetly. "I do wonder," he said, "since these tales come to us through the second wife, whether there are domestic troubles we are not aware of. If the maharajah would consent to an interview without the necessity of bringing to bear the full force of the law . . . I shouldn't care to have this escalate to an international incident.''

"I do understand," Margaret said. "David, am I correct in understanding this other 'wife' is not Indian but a Western woman?''

David looked briefly uneasy. "English," he said. "Doris Smith, she was. Not . . ." he hesitated. "Not someone one would normally meet socially.''

"Ah." Margaret imagined a blue-eyed, peaches-and-cream-complected little London shopgirl who had caught the aging maharajah's eye as he tried to recapture the heyday of the Indian princes. Some, like Ram-Sam, had never come to terms with the idea that kingdoms fall and fade.

David said wearily, "It is a difficult situation. Margaret is here to help convince Highness to take himself and his party to a very fine hotel in London. The Dorchester is open again. The maharajah could think of himself as the guest of the Sultan of Brunei as opposed to a mere earl. And there's always Claridge's. To no avail. Then the murder happened, and now this. . . .''

David indicated a pile of popular London dailies, each with screaming headlines liberally laced with words like "gruesome murder," "foreign royalty," "fortune in gems," and "ancestral home of playboy peer.''

"I'm scarcely a playboy," David said. "And I can't imagine how word got about Fleet Street so quickly. His Highness now says he feels protected from the press here, and he wishes to deal with his tragedy in private. Besides, he likes the Priory. It reminds him of the past. He feels safe.''

"Safe? When his wife was murdered not many yards from this room?" Margaret sank into a chair. "David, I am still existing in another time zone. I need tea and rest." She turned to Westron. "So sorry. I arrived from New York only a few hours ago and drove straight here. Perhaps when I have had a lie-down, I can persuade His Highness to have a serious discussion of recent events. He was always quite fond of me. And . . ." She looked at David.

"I might persuade him to depart, if Mr. Westron will allow it."

"I am somewhat at a loss there," Westron said. "We certainly need to speak with him officially." He was uneasy again. Margaret wondered if he had suspicions about the maharajah's role in this murder. "If you could convince him to meet with me, there are some puzzling matters to be cleared up. The photos of the murder scene . . ." He stopped.

"I should be most interested in seeing them," Margaret said, and knew what sort of look she would have gotten from De Vere at those words. In Sam De Vere's view, Lady Margaret should never, never have anything to do with a murder.

"That won't be necessary, Lady Margaret," Westron said quickly.

"You'd be wise to reconsider, Inspector," David said. "My sister is quite an expert on murder. Never baffled for long." He contemplated a tabloid whose headlines proclaimed: "Country House Murder. Did the Ghost Do It?" In smaller type: "Police Baffled." A grainy archival photo of a young Ram-Sam in full polo gear filled out the front page.

"Never baffled?" Westron took a closer look at Margaret.

"It was entirely chance that I became involved in a murder case," she said. "Once or twice, that is. I'd like to see the photos."

"Really not necessary." But he was weakening.

"Ah, Inspector. Humor me." Margaret turned on all her fine-tuned charm.

"She's right, Inspector," David said. He was becoming impatient. "We need to clear this up at once. You cannot imagine how difficult it is to harbor the Indians and at the same time try to earn a few miserable pounds to keep this place going. And now this murder." The calm facade seemed to be cracking.

"Be patient, David. Mr. Westron will sort things out," Margaret said. She gave him her most charming smile. "What has become of the body, may I ask?"

"We will release it shortly," Westron said. "It's the usual

conclusion with ongoing investigations: person or persons unknown. We are being careful.''

''I do hope we don't discover that the maharajah murdered his wife,'' Margaret said. Westron contrived to look surprised that such a thought had occurred to her. ''He is rather quaint, but entirely charming. Of course, I know nothing of the other wife. Is she prone to murder, do you suppose?''

''Doris—she calls herself Devi now—is a collection of desirable body parts,'' David answered unexpectedly. ''Quite a jolly girl, actually, in spite of low beginnings. She's quite pleased that she's made it to her present lofty state. That's about all I can say of her.'' David met Margaret's eyes briefly and looked away. He was not a good liar.

''Say, Earl, are we going to get to work or what?'' Quintus Roach appeared abruptly on the top step into the vaulted room. ''I've got a pricey film crew waiting. Time is money.''

David stood up. ''Mr. Roach, have you met Mr. Westron from Scotland Yard?''

''Scotland Yard? No kidding? I always wanted to meet someone from the Yard. I remember seeing these English movies . . . Well, it's a step up from the cops I talked to before. I hope you settle this murder soon. Jazmin is raising hell about it. It upsets her spiritual well-being. Karma, serenity, all that California New Age stuff. I never went for it, but it keeps her happy.''

''I shall want to speak with you, Mr. Roach,'' Westron said, ''but naturally your business must proceed.''

''Okay, later,'' Roach said. ''The cameraman wants to set up for the morning light tomorrow, and he needs to get the cherry picker in place to shoot the polo scenes.''

''Polo?'' Margaret thought she must have misheard Roach.

''Not really,'' David said. ''Something that looks like a chukker with shots of the lovely Jazmin gazing adoringly at a space to be occupied by the hero, who will be filmed elsewhere, as I understand it. The maharajah volunteered to ride and act as technical adviser, but I don't know if he will turn up now. If you'll excuse us, Inspector, Mr. Roach and I will be on our way.'' Westron nodded, and David said soothingly,

"I'll look into everything, Roach." The prospect of an en-larged bank account turned the Earl of Brayfield uncharac-teristically ingratiating to a member of the lower orders.

"Are we going to have a problem with power?" Roach said. "The gaffer—whaddya call them here? Chief electri-cian? Anyhow, he's worried."

"We have auxiliary generators," David said soothingly. He looked back at Margaret. "Handle everything, will you? That's a good girl."

Chapter 5

"*What a* mess to come home to," Margaret said. She was beginning to feel extraordinarily weary, but she wanted a look at those murder scene photos.

"The alleged intruder," Westron began, but Margaret waved that possibility away briskly.

Westron relented. "This is perhaps not as simple an affair as I indicated earlier." He spoke reluctantly. "I have instructions to treat the maharajah gently. All the same . . ." He sighed. "We cannot fix a precise time of the attack on the lady. We do not know the whereabouts exactly of the people who were present in this house during the evening and after dinner. As your brother noted, they had scattered by the time the lady was probably murdered. We certainly have no evidence of a break-in."

"So," Margaret said slowly, "that it might have been her husband, or this other wife or one of the other guests, or heaven forbid, even my brother."

"Opportunity," Westron mumbled uneasily. "And motive. We tend to look first at . . . intimates. This Doris . . ." He stopped, and flipped open a small black notebook. "A girl from the country who did well for herself, according to some lights. We have interviewed everyone except for the maharajah and Nigel Priam, who moved on to London that night and has not yet been located. We have yet to speak to the Indian servants, who are engaged in mourning rituals, but we'll be talking to them. It has been difficult to get solid information. No one knows anything, although more than one of your household staff have muttered about these two ghosts.''

"We do have rather more than our share," Margaret said absently, "but they don't stab people. I don't know that Scotland Yard would be willing to share information with me. . . . " She did not miss the slight narrowing of the eyes, the muscle that twitched in his cheek, the frown loaded with doubt. She had seen the same look all too often on De Vere's face, just before he said very firmly that he did not wish her to become involved in a murder.

"I should not care for you to become involved in a murder, Lady Margaret," Westron said.

"But people will talk to me," Margaret said. "People of . . . well, my class. And the people who serve my class. I am Lady Margaret, not a policeman. As you say, we must tread carefully."

"It's not a question of who stole the buns. It's murder."

"Inspector, allow me to tell you about me and murder. And about a friend who is an American policeman."

Not long after, she and Westron had come to a tentative understanding, and Westron brought out the glossy black-and-white photos of the murder scene. In the glare of the flashes, the dark-haired maharani in her elaborate sari was a frail, tragic figure. Margaret saw the splashes of blood from the cut on her hand and arm, but could not see how she had died.

"The fatal injury to the heart did not cause much external bleeding," Westron said. "She apparently attempted to fend off her killer with her right hand, she was cut by the murder weapon, and that caused the mess. Oh, and her garment was slightly damp, so we assume that she entered this Nun's Walk from the outside rather than through the house. The rain started around eleven."

"She must have seen him or her," Margaret said half to herself. "What sort of knife, I wonder."

"We have not found it. It appears that it was not an ordinary sort of blade.'' Westron was still hesitant about sharing official information with Margaret.

''You are saying then that she was not stabbed with a run-of-the-mill kitchen knife. Well, we have cabinets full of weaponry about the place, collected by military Priams over the centuries.''

''Lord Brayfield accompanied the local people to the places around the house where various old weapons are displayed, but none of them appear to have gone missing,'' he said cautiously. ''Your Mrs. Domby showed us the kitchen knives. We have not . . .'' He stopped.

''Asked His Highness,'' Margaret finished for him. ''And I judge that this Doris denies possessing any sort of dagger.'' She took up the pictures again. ''And what do the police experts make of these?'' Margaret pointed to the neat series of bloody handprints on the light-colored stone floor of the corridor near the maharani's body.

''She seems not to have died immediately. She must have reached out her injured hand to raise herself, or to crawl along the passageway to reach this room.''

''Very clear, aren't they?'' Margaret said. ''Almost too purposeful to be accidental.'' Margaret was thoughtful. She imagined the maharani gliding along the Nun's Walk, silently pursued by a village lad bent on robbery, or by a professional thief who had heard rumors of fabulous wealth in the maharajah's possession. No, that wasn't right. No one would look for a treasure in the Nun's Walk. But if it was someone from the house, one of the people who had supposedly departed after dinner, a person seeking her, a face she recognized as the dagger struck her . . .

''I beg your pardon, Lady Margaret.'' She recognized Harbert, although he was much changed in the few years since she had last seen him. Heavier and more serious if that was possible, although still a comparatively young man. He was formally attired, no doubt in honor of the somber events at the Priory. His long face was grave, but that was his normal look. ''I regret that I was not at the door to welcome you. Your room has been prepared. Mrs. Domby is having tea sent up.''

"Thank you, Harbert. What sort of schedule does Highness keep? I would like to . . . to arrange an audience." Margaret recalled that the maharajah retained a taste for formality, especially in small matters related to his former status. Old habits die hard, and none die harder than those involved with the trappings of imagined privilege.

"He keeps his own schedule," Harbert said sourly. "I shall have a message sent up. Perhaps the surviving so-called maharani can arrange it." He withdrew with almost a bow in Margaret's direction and no notice at all of Westron.

"Well!" Margaret said. "Quite unlike the Harbert I remember. Most unusual for him to make such a comment before an outsider."

Westron managed a faint smile. He consulted his notebook. "Richard Harbert, employed here for six years, four months. According to your brother, he had excellent references from Sir Henry Blitworth. He was the tinned meat man, wasn't he? Unmarried. Occupies rooms on the top floor. Said by his lordship to be honest, diligent, et cetera, et cetera. He states that the house had been made secure before he retired. Very reticent to speak ill of his lordship's houseguests, but is clearly disapproving of both the film people and the Indians. Like me, Mr. Harbert is perhaps somewhat affronted by the high-handed treatment meted out by Mr. R. Tharpur, citizen of India."

"Oh, no," Margaret said. "Harbert is a total snob. Once a king, always a king, whatever a man's government decides to call him. I believe Harbert would allow Highness whatever whim he fancies, although I'm sure that retinue of servants has ruffled him. In the old days when Highness came to stay with us, he never brought more than one personal servant—I do not include the grooms and trainers who handled his polo ponies, and the man who cared for the equipment."

Margaret stood up and moved her shoulders to ease their tightness. "I really must rest," she said. "I came here at my brother's summons to persuade His Highness to remove himself and leave David and the Priory in peace, but I do not care for our guests being slaughtered under our roof. It isn't done. I don't like to see the Priam name damaged."

"We all have our priorities," Westron said. "Mine is strictly murder."

"But in aid of our good name, I may discover something to aid in your priority," Margaret said. She did not add that in spite of her promises to De Vere, she was indeed sufficiently offended by the idea of a murder occurring at Priam's Priory that she was determined to see that the affair was resolved, with or without the aid of the bland and diplomatic Mr. Westron.

Surely De Vere would understand that—if she ever had the chance to explain.

Margaret made her way to the floor above via the narrow stairs in the corner of the morning room, which overlooked the lawns. At the top of the staircase was a tall oriel window with diamond-shaped panes and a seat in the embrasure for contemplation of the distant low hills beyond the woods. Her old room was the first on the left, and beyond it were more bedrooms—including the distressingly uncomfortable Queen's Bedroom—ending with David's own suite of rooms above the drive. Another long hall at right angles to this one led to the wing inhabited by the maharajah's entourage—small bedrooms, baths, and sitting rooms and another large suite corresponding to David's that would be Ram-Sam's personal quarters for the duration of his visit.

As she approached her room, she smelled the heavy, sweet incense that had drifted down the hall from the Indians' wing, and she thought she saw the edge of a bright sari disappear through one of the distant doors. She sniffed. There was a faint spicy odor about as well that suggested that the Indian ladies were continuing to cook in one of the old fireplaces, in spite of Mrs. Domby.

She pondered for a moment before she entered her room. The maharani had been caught by the rain on her way to the Nun's Walk, so she had left the house by one of several doors. She could have descended by the main staircase near His Highness's suite, or used the stairs Margaret had just taken, or the back stairs from the Indian encampment, which led to the mud room and the estate offices. Perhaps she had gone outside because any route through the house risked an encounter with someone off to bed or roaming about looking for a splash of whiskey before retiring. There was another stairway, but it was private, from David's quarters down to the ground floor room that was now a pantry off the kitchen. That route allowed one to pass through the kitchen to a door that gave entrance to the Nun's Walk and to the enclosed garden.

She tried to imagine the maharani creeping through the rainy night on an urgent visit to her husband. Did she sense a watcher in the trees or behind the low brick wall of the garden? When she hastened along the Nun's Walk, had she come upon someone who knew that the royal lady's nighttime excursion would cause trouble too great to be explained away? Perhaps someone with a motive for her death who had merely been waiting for the opportunity . . .

What, indeed, had been her mission?

Margaret was too travel-weary to think in an orderly manner. She wished to lie down and let her questions sift themselves out in her unconscious mind. As she entered her room, a door far away in the Indian wing opened, and she heard a gabble of high-pitched voices speaking an incomprehensible tongue. There was a burst of sound, like wails of grief. Then the door was closed, and silence returned. How many women, she wondered, did the maharajah have in tow to mourn his dead lady?

She was pleased to find that the room where she had spent the years prior to her brief marriage—after being finished off at a school in Switzerland and during extended stays when she was doing an art course in London—was little changed. She and her mother had chosen the decor: delicate chintz fabrics with a rosy color predominating, a high four-poster bed with a heavy lace and chintz canopy and draperies tied back at the corners, and a pile of pillows. The main windows had a view of the lawn, and three smaller windows on the adjoining wall looked down on the roofs of David's old priory room and the Nun's Walk, and on the beautiful old walled garden, which at this season was lush with blossoms and greenery. One could even catch sight of the little stone fountain in the corner of the garden where she had played jungle explorer and captive princess under the overgrown bushes.

A pot of tea had been set out on the table in front of the windows. Margaret drank a cup with rich cream from the estate farm, then bathed to wash away the smell of recirculated airplane air, and put on a robe to rest for an hour or two. Tilda, the maid, had managed to contain her hysteria over the discovery of a murdered woman, and had unpacked Margaret's clothes and put them away. Even without a mistress in the house, Priam's Priory still ran on the strict lines set down by her mother and her grandmother.

She closed her eyes, and saw in her mind's eye the photos of the maharani with the bloody handprints. Margaret was certain that the dead maharani had intended to send a last message to the living.

So many people she had to talk to—this Doris of Tharpur, David's girlfriend, Chloe, the film people, the new American neighbors, the maharajah. And what about Nigel? At the thought of her cousin, she opened her eyes, and caught sight of the little painting of a long-ago Countess of Brayfield that hung on her wall. A great-great-great aunt who had died childless, so that the title passed eventually to the then-earl's brother, finally reaching her own dear, distracted brother. That would be the course of modern history if David failed to marry and produce a male heir who would be raised to love the old Priory as David and Margaret did. If something happened to David tomorrow, the title and the Priory would pass to her father's younger brother, old Uncle Lawrence, living out his retirement in a modest little house in Surrey, surrounded by memories of his Indian service. After that— horrors—all would pass to his son Nigel.

She never thought of such things back in New York. Never. Nigel was a rogue, entirely unsuited to the responsibilities of this place. She felt her eyes grow heavy with transoceanic weariness, too strong to allow the twinge of uneasiness she felt to keep her awake. Nigel and the title. Nigel and his disgraceful escapades and unflappable good nature. Nigel here the night of the murder.

The handprints, the weapon that was not an ordinary knife, the ghosts that roam when there's trouble afoot.

Margaret slept.

Chapter 6

Suddenly, without knowing how much time had passed,
Margaret was awake, but she willed herself not to move, not
to open her eyes. The creak of the door opening gently and
the rustle of fabric told her that someone had come into her
room, likely a female and not very likely one of the servants.
If it was not a matter of life and death, the servants would
never intrude unless summoned or at a prearranged hour for
waking.

Margaret lay frozen as soft footsteps passed her bed and
moved toward the windows. There was a faint sound as the
long curtains were drawn back slightly. Then there was silence. The person appeared to have seated herself in one of
the chairs in front of the windows. Definitely not one of the
household staff.

Margaret moved her head as though turning it in her sleep,
and opened one eye a fraction, hoping that her gaze would
fall on her visitor. At the same time, she heard a click, and
smelled the aroma of smoke from a perfumed cigarette. What
she saw was a golden jeweled sandal, with toes lacquered a
gleaming red. She saw the edge of a yellow garment heavily
embroidered with an intricate design in many colors.

An Indian lady, certainly. Margaret was still in the final
throes of travel-induced lethargy. She decided to wait as she

was, continue her refreshing period of recovery, and see what happened next.

"You can open your eyes now," a woman's voice said. "I know you're awake." It was an English voice, but not an upper-class accent, although it strove to be. It was certainly not an Indian voice, even one richly overlaid with the tones of the raj. Cautiously Margaret shifted and opened her eyes wide while raising herself up on one elbow.

If she was not mistaken, Margaret had in her view David's "collection of desirable body parts," the alleged surviving Maharani of Tharpur. She was a handsome woman rather than a beauty, not at all the rosy-cheeked slip of a girl Margaret had imagined. She would be quite tall when she stood, and she wore her honey-blond hair in a sleek chignon. She displayed a certain languid poise in the entirely at-ease pose she struck as she lounged in the chair. She smoked her perfumed cigarette in a long mother-of-pearl holder, and her arms were covered from wrist to elbow with bangles heavy with bits of colored stones, possibly the real thing.

A bit much, Margaret thought, especially with those earrings.

"You must be Doris," Margaret said without thinking.

The woman leaned her head to one side and flicked the ashes from her cigarette onto the rug.

"Doris is dead," she said. "I am Her Highness Devi, the Maharani of Tharpur."

Hold on a bit, my girl, Margaret thought as she sat up and swung her legs over the side of the bed. Then she slipped down the considerable distance to the floor.

"And I am Lady Margaret Priam," she said. "Not dead, not yet. May I ask why you have invaded my private quarters?"

Doris-Devi stood up and opened wide the long curtains that had blocked out the midday light while Margaret dozed.

Doris—Margaret chose to think of her as such until convinced it should be otherwise—whirled about in her flowing sari so that she stood with her back to Margaret, looking out on the Priam estate. Doris did not answer Margaret's question. Instead she said, "David said that you were here. He said I could trust you."

Ah, David, is it? Margaret thought, and waited.

"He said you're tight with the copper from the Yard."

"Not precisely," Margaret said. News traveled very fast through Priam's Priory. "I spoke briefly with Mr. Westron. I've only just arrived."

"They're always out to spoil a girl's bit of fun," Doris said petulantly. She suddenly seemed young and rebellious rather than assured and queenly. Margaret guessed that she was a bit past her mid-twenties. The maharajah was decades older.

"You haven't yet told me the reason for your visit," Margaret said.

"I need your help," Doris said. "The police suspect me, I know it, but I had nothing to do with killing off that bloody old woman. I wouldn't say we were chums exactly, but we didn't have any quarrel. I almost never saw her, not here, not in India." She wrinkled her nose in distaste in naming the country. "I told the police that it could just as easily have been me that died, don't you think?"

"I don't know what to think," Margaret said. "Who would want to murder you?"

Doris was flustered momentarily. "A robber after my jewels! I have a lot of good stones with me. Everybody knows that. It *could* have been me that was dead instead of her. Who could tell the difference?"

"Someone attacked a woman in a sari believing it was you rather than Her Highness?" Margaret knew she sounded skeptical.

Doris was losing her poise. "A bit o' that, it might be," she said. "Lady Margaret, I'm frightened. Ram says it's agents of the government after him, but that's nonsense. They don't care a bit about him, but it makes him feel important. I know it's some crazy person after me who doesn't like foreigners."

Margaret was astonished. "But you're not a foreigner. Not in England, in any case."

But how greatly might Ram-Sam's other ladies and servants and retainers loathe the idea of an Englishwoman lording it over them, someone who was one of the hated former—and foreign—rulers of their land? "Are you thinking of the Indians?"

"I don't know what to think," Doris said. "I'm frightened. That Indian crowd never liked me, and now they're sitting around on the floor crying and moaning about her like they lost their mum. Ram has scarcely had a word for me since it happened."

Margaret did not feel up to measuring the bonds forged by a long marriage and shared ancient traditions against a fling with a pretty young woman.

"He's the way he gets when it suits him to go all native," Doris said.

"I beg your pardon?"

"When he does all the things he's always done back there in dreary old Tharpur." She lapsed into a fairly good imitation of an Indian accent. "We are looking at the bir'day parade. Oh, my goodness yes, they are very fine elephants indeed. We are having tea and sweeties on the balcony while we are watching. Jolly good . . ." She wrinkled her nose. "You know, the ceremonies and audiences, and that crumbling old palace he won't let me modernize. There's the religious business I don't understand at all. And send the women away when any interesting men pay a call. It's an awfully old-fashioned place. Worse than I imagined."

Margaret wondered if Doris was about to explain how good it all sounded at first on a damp, rainy day in London when a rich if aging Indian prince promised her hot, sunny India with all the jewels she desired and servants falling all over themselves, and palaces galore. A royal title to boot, even if it didn't count and there was the slight inconvenience of an existing wife.

Doris was pacing back and forth before the windows. She carried herself stiffly, as though the elegant sari was still an uncomfortable make-believe costume.

"I imagined," Doris said, "that it would set me up for good and give me a whole new life. Better than what I had."

"Only it was a different kind of life altogether than what you'd expected."

"Right. You wouldn't understand. You were born with a name and a title and this house. You've never had to change who you are or forget the past." She seemed to draw back into herself. "I wish we hadn't come here," she said. "I begged to stay in London, but Ram insisted. Now, Ram is very, very fond of me. Don't be mistaken about that. We lead a very Western sort of life when it's the two of us. I know he likes pretty women about, but that's nothing, is it? We've traveled all over Europe and stayed at the best hotels. I have as many servants as I'll ever need, and he pays for everything I want."

"And the marriage? I mean the legal aspects."

Doris shrugged. "What wasn't quite . . . right before will be right soon enough, now that she's gone. But . . ." There was desperation in her eyes. "Can you help me? Tell them I didn't do it?"

"Doris, I'd never wish anyone to be accused of a murder she didn't commit, but you do have a good motive," Margaret said. "And telling tales to the police about government plots isn't going to help your cause." She began to look through her clothes, to decide who it was she was likely to be seeing and what would be deemed appropriate.

"I never did any such thing! I mean to say, I only repeated what Ram told me. And I was asleep when it happened. I must have been, since I went right up to my rooms after sitting about for a bit with those people who dined. We had coffee, and then those Americans decided to push off, and Nigel just a bit later."

"I suppose the police have asked if anyone can verify your whereabouts."

"His Highness could do so if he chose," Doris said grandly, but she would not meet Margaret's eye. "He is not seeing anyone."

"He will be seeing me, I think," Margaret said. "After I've dressed and had a private chat with my brother."

"He will not speak to anyone."

"He will arrange a few minutes with me," Margaret said

very firmly, "or Scotland Yard will descend on him in all its might. Please see to it, or I shall simply appear and will not be turned away."

Doris continued to gaze out on the lawns. "All right. I'll speak to him. He's talked about you. The way your mum welcomed him in the old days. I've heard all about this house, but I never thought to be here." She drew herself up proudly. "Never mind, I can take care of myself. You know, I dreamt of this greenness when I was stuck out there in India in the middle of the desert. Those poor, miserable women kicking up the dust along the roads, and bent over in their poor little fields, and all those cows in the streets." Doris had obviously not been charmed by the peculiar magic of India.

"You could leave him, you know," Margaret said.

"Impossible," Doris said sharply. "There's plenty of reasons not to."

"I do wonder why Highness decided to hole up at Priam's Priory," Margaret asked casually. "It's not exactly the Dorchester."

Doris turned around and faced Margaret. "There's the film, of course."

"Not the Quintus Roach film surely."

"That one," Doris said. "Ram has put money into it. He has a lot of investments. Your cousin Nigel got him interested because of the polo business."

"Nigel!"

"Well, you know, he's an old chum of mine, and since you have the polo field and the house, Ram was keen on the whole business. Then there was . . ." She narrowed her eyes. It was a look Margaret recognized: a woman mentally confronting the potential Other Woman. Jazmin Burns was as blond as the art of hair styling could make her, and—as David had noted—His Highness was greatly attracted to blondes. The complications of this simple little murder were beginning to multiply. And then there was more.

"I suppose your brother has told you all about him and me."

Margaret was somehow not totally unprepared. "Whatever do you mean?"

"Well, if he hasn't mentioned it . . . I'd best be going to fix up your meeting with Ram."

"No," Margaret said. "You'll stay and tell me about you and my brother."

"I knew him in London before I met Ram. I used to live in a deadly little village on the edge of the North Sea. Definitely not for me, so I went to London. That was going to be more like really living."

"And it wasn't?"

"I was just looking for fun and wanting to get away from a bad life," Doris said. "It's always been hard. You wouldn't know about that. I admit I've made some mistakes. The wrong man, and when he left, he promised to send for me. You know what that's worth. So I did what I had to do, and no looking back."

"And there in London, you came upon my brother and Nigel."

"I started to go about to parties and clubs, Annabel's and places like that. Nigel introduced me to David; you know how things happen." She hesitated. "Nigel was quite taken with me, even if he was a bit of a bounder. But I knew he came from a nice family. He was all right, he taught me a few things about how to behave, how to talk to people. He even took me to visit his dad. Lovely old gentleman; we hit it off grand. Well, I had to make something of myself, didn't I? It's not like you. You can have any man you want."

Margaret doubted that, thinking of the distant Sam De Vere.

"David and me had some good times. He helped fix me up with a job at a bank. Ram's London bank, in fact, and since David had known him for ages, one thing led to another. . . . "

"So it seems," Margaret said. She did not trust in the truth of Doris's tale, but now there was something more that she needed to discuss with her brother. She took clothing into her large bathroom so as to give herself a breathing space while she dressed. Light trousers and a silk shirt in case she found herself tramping over the estate or driving about in the Land Rover. She came back into the bedroom.

"I haven't felt at all well since I've been here," Doris said wanly, making a stab at gaining sympathy. "One of the maids said it was because the ghosts don't take to me."

"*Utter* nonsense." Margaret could hear the impatience in her own voice. "We have two entirely harmless apparitions. The old nun goes back many centuries, and the gray lady was said to have been murdered by her husband in the nineteenth century around the time of Napoleon. Someone wrote it up in a book we have in the library. The nun is kindly, and the other seems merely to enjoy terrifying people."

Doris did not speak again, so Margaret turned from the mirror where she was fixing her hair to look at her. She was staring at her hands, turning her very large—not to say gaudy—rings that were probably part of the Tharpur treasure trove. Then she said, "There was said to be a ghost in the big house near our village. Someone I knew said he saw it once. Nearly scared him to death. He was only the gamekeeper's assistant then, but he was full of big tales. A good-looking man with grand fancies trying to impress me." She chuckled bitterly. "And he did. Have you ever seen your ghosts?"

"I saw the nun once when I was ten or eleven, near what is now David's priory room. It was half-ruined then, with damp dirt floors and shaky columns, and I wasn't allowed to go there, but I did. She was just a faint outline, but I knew right away it was her. Others have seen the murdered gray lady or sensed her. A presence, footsteps when there was no one about, a feeling of coldness and grief. Very different types as ghosts go."

"Do they share the same space, these two different women?"

"What? Oh no, if I understand you. They haunt different parts of the house. Quite separate lives, as it were."

At last Doris moved toward the door. "I shall convince Ram to see you. After lunch. Come to his suite about three. I have the large room next to it. The old wife was at the end of the hall. I never knew what she did with herself all day." She opened the door of Margaret's room and found herself face-to-face with Harbert, whose hand was raised to knock.

"Lady Margaret, so sorry to trouble you," Harbert said, pointedly ignoring Doris. "Inspector Westron wishes to see you urgently on a matter of importance. May I tell him that you will join him in the library presently?"

"Yes," Margaret said.

Harbert started to withdraw and paused. "Madam," he said sternly to Doris, "your servants have been cooking in their rooms again. See that it ceases." He turned on his heel and departed.

"Listen to him, will you?" Doris said. "Doesn't he put on airs? He forgets to whom he is speaking." She glanced nervously at Margaret, as if to see if she had handled a grand English servant properly. Margaret's smile was soothing, and she forbore to mention that Doris's airs were quite as remarkable.

"Doesn't know his place," Doris said haughtily, and swept out, almost slamming the door behind her.

Margaret stared thoughtfully at the door. She was sure that it had occurred to Doris that many people, including the police, might think that the elimination of an inconvenient wife was an entirely logical reason for murder.

Margaret ran a comb through her hair and prepared to descend for her meeting with Westron. She opened the door a sliver to be sure the coast was clear of English peers, Indian maharanis, and affronted servants. She stepped back quickly. At the junction of the two hallways, Doris could be seen, but not heard, in a heated conversation with Harbert. It seemed to be her turn to berate him, while he listened stoically. Then Doris turned on her bejeweled heel and flounced away toward the Indian wing, apparently the winner in the dialogue between master and servant classes. Harbert watched her depart, then headed for the stairs down to the ground floor.

Let us hope, Margaret thought as she prepared to follow Harbert, that in the end, some lout from a distant village is found with the stolen necklace and confesses all. Although logic suggested that none of the occupants and neighbors of Priam's Priory were prone to murderous behavior, it would be a relief to be sure.

"Lady Margaret . . ." Harbert was hovering at the foot

of the stairs. "I must explain my unforgivable behavior just now."

"Nothing to explain," Margaret said graciously.

"I shouldn't wonder if you reported my rudeness to one of our guests to Lord Brayfield. I don't know what came over me. She is only a girl of the lower classes who gives herself airs, but I had no cause to speak to her as I did."

"Don't worry." Margaret was soothing. "I understand how trying it must be to have the maharajah here, and all his people. I shan't mention it to my brother."

"Thank you." Harbert was positively humble. "It won't happen again. Inspector Westron is in the library, with . . ." He hesitated.

"Yes?"

"With Mr. Priam. Mr. Nigel Priam. The local constable just brought him round from the pub."

Chapter 7

"*Well, well,* cousin Maggie." Nigel Priam was sprawled in a big leather chair with his feet up on a hassock. The library was a dark room, impressively lined with floor-to-ceiling bookcases filled with volumes collected over centuries by the Priams. Margaret's nineteenth-century great-grandfather had been an avid book collector, and her grandfather had added to the collections. Her own father had been rather more interested in sport than books. The room had undergone many transformations since the house was built, and now was more Victorian than anything else, with a heavy, scholarly air about it.

"What a surprise to find you here, Nigel," Margaret said. "I understood you'd been and gone in a flash."

"Right enough," Nigel said. "And now I'm back." He grinned. He was about Margaret's age, in his mid-thirties, with dark, wavy hair and handsome but somewhat petulant features. He was only a few years older than David, but time and/or extensive frolicking had taken a toll on Nigel.

"I discover," Nigel said, "that this dear man from Scotland Yard has a few questions for me." Westron stood with his back to them, gazing at a shelf of Dickens first editions. "Imagine a murder at Priam's Priory! What would Aunt Elizabeth have said at such a turn of events?"

Margaret thought that her late mother would have looked

disapproving, and then would have gotten on with the business of the day. But it was hard to imagine murder daring to intrude on the Countess of Brayfield's routine.

Westron turned around to face them. "I do have a few questions, Mr. Priam," he said, "although I did not know I would have the opportunity to ask them so soon. A matter of you discovered attempting to sell a few rather valuable bits of jewelry in London yesterday. Identified as of Indian origin."

"My dear Inspector," Nigel said, and stood up. "I have quite a reasonable explanation. I needed money, so I decided to sell something that would bring me money. Nothing wrong in that."

"The murdered lady, the Maharani of Tharpur, was said to have been wearing jewelry, but there was none when her body was found," Westron said.

"I assure you, I do not murder ladies for their jewelry, no matter what their ethnic origin. And what I was selling was nothing to speak of. Some pieces acquired in India years ago."

Margaret seldom felt inclined to defend her cousin, but now she was compelled for the sake of the family name to offer an explanation. "My uncle Lawrence, Nigel's father, spent a good deal of time in India as a young man, in the Indian Civil Service. He was actually posted to Tharpur right before independence, and stayed on for a time. He brought back some lovely things, including jewels presented to him by Ram-Sam. That is to say, Highness has always been most generous." She was eyeing Nigel, who merely smiled blandly. Margaret had no doubt that Nigel wouldn't hesitate to appropriate some of his father's little treasures to support his indolent life-style. All the Priams knew he liked gambling at the London clubs, wagering at the track, toying with expensive women, and all the other pricey appurtenances of roguish upper-class life.

"I do thank you for your support, Maggie," Nigel said, "but I should confess right now. Inspector, those tawdry jewels were not, strictly speaking, mine to sell, but they do belong to my family. I am sure my father understands the necessity—"

"There's the matter of the newspapers," Westron began, and Nigel had the good grace to look somewhat shamefaced.

"Newspapers?" Margaret asked in alarm.

"I said I needed money," Nigel said, "and the press chaps were quite taken with the tale of a former maharani struck down at the home of the handsome young earl. . . . "

"You didn't!" Margaret said. "How could you?"

"And how did you know?" Westron said. "You had departed."

"I knew because I rang up the next morning. Harbert told me all about it, and it occurred to me that my press friends would be interested, for a price. I say, Maggie, have you glimpsed that splendid creature from the depths of Hollywood, United States of America? I manage to get by on very little when necessary, but if one wishes to make a significant impression on the likes of Jazmin Burns, one requires the wherewithal."

"Jazmin Burns?" Margaret knew she sounded somewhat shrill. "And you? How absurd!"

"Not terribly," Nigel said cheerfully. "She's under the impression that I am some sort of wealthy nobleman. I tried to explain that David is the peer, and I am not even an Honourable, but to no avail. She thinks of me as a probable and willing conquest. David is ruffled by that. Fancies her a bit himself, but it's always been David's way to compete with me. Do you remember how we used to escape from him by crawling out through the attics onto the roofs of the Priory amongst the chimney pots? And we'd hide in the ruins and pretend we were the ghosts. You must have been ten or twelve. David would tell tales on us to Aunt Elizabeth because we wouldn't take him along. Too dangerous for the little heir."

"I remember," Margaret murmured. She wanted to ask him about David and Doris and himself in London, but dared not speak of it within the hearing of Scotland Yard.

"Mr. Priam," Westron said. "I wonder if you could find

a place to contemplate what are probably your many sins,
until I have time to speak with you?''

Nigel half bowed. ''My pleasure, sir. Indeed, I am now
staying here in the house. I have a favorite corner, way up
on the top floor where the servants live. Mrs. Domby has
settled me in. She's always been a bit soft about me. There's
a lovely view of the estate from up there, although it is a bit
like Satan taking Jesus up to the mountain and tempting him.
You must remember the vicar's sermon on the subject, Maggie. I never understood why the Lord turned the offer down.
All those glorious acres.'' He winked and went to the double
door of the library. ''I should state that I was captured by the
coppers while talking to Ted at the Riming Man and chatting
up the locals. The topic *du jour* was the murder, and second,
these Americans David sold the manor to. Name of Flood.
They bought Rime Manor. They've got pots of money, I
understand, and the breadth of vision to send some of it
Priamwards. Lucky David.'' Nigel had a look of satisfaction
that made Margaret just a touch wary. Then he was gone.

''Some might see him as a very appealing young man,''
Westron said. He was almost smiling. ''I imagine he has
quite the way with the ladies, although I can't help thinking
he's memorized the lines of some disreputable relative from
some flimsy drawing room comedy.''

''You surely don't suspect him of murdering Her Highness,'' Margaret said, ''although I am rather cross that he
sold information to the press.''

''We have no idea of his whereabouts at the time of her
death, but there's the matter of that jewelry.''

''I have no doubt that Nigel would take anything lying
about Uncle Lawrence's house if he needed it. Perhaps you
should inquire of Nigel's father if anything's gone missing.''

''We are,'' Westron said shortly, and did not elaborate.

''Harbert said that you wished to see me,'' she began.

''One question, Lady Margaret.'' Westron gestured for
her to sit. She now saw that the long library table had been
cleared of its usual copies of *Tatler*, *Harpers & Queen*, and
the *Illustrated London News*, and had become a sort of work-

table for the police. "You looked at the photos of the murdered woman, and you asked about the bloody handprints."

Margaret nodded.

"While you were resting, I managed to speak to one of the Indian ladies who are here as the servants of the maharajah's party, and showed her the photos. She became quite agitated, but I was unable to get any explanation, either from her or from an elderly gentleman with quite good English who appears to be the maharajah's personal servant. Now, I do need to know what significance you find in the handprints."

Margaret thought about how to answer. "I had an intuition when I saw the photos," she said. "Something I remembered from my visit to Tharpur. Perhaps the Indian lady has confirmed my first thought, although it may not be correct. It seems to indicate clearly that it was not a break-in and robbery, but a personal attack on the maharani."

Westron waited.

"When I visited Rajasthan—Tharpur and the cities of the old princes in the desert, Jaipur and Udaipur and the rest," Margaret said, "I was shown walls covered with handprints left by Hindu widows who chose to sacrifice themselves on their dead husbands' funeral pyres. To become sati. It's a custom that's been outlawed for ages, but it's still occasionally practiced. The tradition is certainly still part of common lore. The problem of what to do with women who no longer have husbands continues to be an issue in India. I understand that sati is still viewed as an heroic act, even when a family is glad to rid itself of the burden of a widow and perhaps get back her dowry. Please don't ask me to analyze the motivations."

"You are suggesting that as a traditional wife, the maharani—as she was being murdered—tried to leave a message? Even as she was dying, she wanted to tell her husband that he was—is—in danger so great that it could have left her a widow had she been alive to see it. . . . "

"Something like that," Margaret said. "Something that might only harm him. It does sound far-fetched."

"Not entirely, I think. His position is that he is worried

about his own safety. This might, however, be purely a diversionary tactic.'' He did not actually say that Ram-Sam was also a likely suspect. ''It is imperative that someone speak to His Highness.''

''I think I shall be allowed this afternoon,'' Margaret said. ''I have put in a word with . . .'' How to refer to Doris? Her Highness, his wife, the maharani, or simply Doris? ''With the Englishwoman. Do you know anything further of her antecedents?'' The inspector had not mentioned any knowledge of her brother's previous acquaintance with Doris, Nigel had uncharacteristically remained silent about that old connection, and Margaret was not going to speak of it until she had talked with David.

Westron blinked and said only, ''We are continuing our investigations. Kindly see me as soon as you have spoken to the maharajah. We are not asking you to extract information from him,'' he said severely, in case she had forgotten. He was instructing her clearly not to do any ''investigating'' of her own. ''We ask you simply to persuade him that it is in his best interests to allow us to interview him as soon as possible.'' Westron looked at his watch. ''I am expecting Mr. Roach, as he promised to complete his preparations for filming by lunchtime. He seems to feel he has information of use to the police.''

''Does he indeed?'' Margaret said. ''I should judge that he would be much more interested in buying the story rights to the true-life drama taking place before his eyes.''

Chapter 8

*D*avid *was* going to sit down now and explain to her about knowing Doris and where he was when the maharani was stabbed, how much the Floods had paid for the manor, and whether his current girlfriend, Chloe Waters, was a homicidal maniac. The police were not going to forget about David as a suspect just because he held an ancient title. Margaret marched out of the library.

Now that she was alone and comparatively alert, she could not rcsist the desire to peer into some of the ground-floor rooms of the house. The sight of them stirred up those fond memories that had haunted her since she had arrived. How grateful she was that David continued to struggle to keep the Priory going. She was almost certain that she would stay on for a time, and forget about De Vere and New York. First she would try to help clear up this unfortunate death, which was only a little blip on the screen of Priam history, and then all would be well.

She opened the door to the large drawing room. It was seldom used, but the successful restoration her mother had accomplished after the war had stood up well. The sun shone in on the old and valuable Priam furniture, mixed with comfortable modern pieces. The Chinese porcelain figure of Kuan Yin from the Boxer Rebellion stood on a fine antique table, and some Mogul miniatures given to the Priory by Uncle

Lawrence hung on a far wall. As she closed the door, she almost tripped over Wally, who had sniffed her out and wagged his tail at the sight of her.

"Come along, old boy," she said. "Let's see the music room." The so-called music room opening off the long hall was dark. It now was a room without windows, although in earlier times, before additions were built on, it, too, had looked upon the lawns. Since Regency days, it had been occasionally used as a ballroom; the walls covered in yellow silk and the chandelier with hundreds of sparkling crystal droplets made it a dazzling place when filled with snowy bosoms covered with the family gems, and sleek men in black tie. Margaret had had a sort of debutante ball here, and David's twenty-first birthday fête had attracted a huge crowd of upper-class youngsters, distinguished enough for photos to appear in the pages of *Tatler*. Because it had no exterior walls, it was the warmest room in the house in winter when a fire was ablaze in the carved fireplace.

Margaret stepped into the room and squinted into the darkness. The grand piano no one played was a looming shadow. She started to leave, then looked again. The top of a person's head was just visible over the back of an armchair.

"Hullo?" she said tentatively. The head did not move.

Suddenly Wally froze, and she heard him growl deeply. She reached down to stroke him, and felt the hackles that had risen along his back.

"Silly thing," she murmured. "It's nothing to be alarmed about. One of our household is having a private nap." But somehow she knew that it was not a visitor or a servant, not a trick of the light streaming in from the open door behind her, or even someone from the film crew who had crept in and fallen asleep. She decided that she would find out who had intruded.

Margaret walked slowly through the darkness toward the high-backed chair. Wally refused to follow her. All at once, she was aware that she had passed a barrier from the musty warmth of a long-closed room into a circle of cold. She knew she did not imagine that her hands and face felt as though they had been thrust into a ice chest. Her heart started to race.

I will *not* be afraid, she told herself. If this is the ghost, I have met ghosts before and lived to tell the tale. But she felt fingers of terror on her neck. She sensed a wave of utter grief washing over her, and then she took hold of herself. There had been entirely too much wild talk of the ghosts; the power of suggestion had done something to her brain.

"Hullo?" she said again tentatively. Now she wasn't sure she could see the pale head any longer. She continued bravely across the room into deeper gloom as she left the shaft of light from the hall door.

"Ah!" The gasp was involuntary. Whatever she thought she had seen was suddenly gone, and the air she breathed was as warm and musty as when she had entered.

"Did you see it? Wasn't it fabulous?"

Margaret whirled around at the sound of the voice.

Jazmin Burns, instantly recognizable, emerged from a dark corner of the room. She was got up in hunting scarlet, although Margaret was certain that no one had designated her a Master of the Hunt. She might have been attempting to blend into the country scene, or she may have believed she was costumed for her film role. Margaret wondered in passing if Quintus Roach had somehow confused polo and fox hunting in his script. At least there was a common link in the fact that horses were required for both sports.

"I'm not sure I saw anything," Margaret said cautiously. "You must be Miss Burns. I am Margaret Priam, David's sister."

"Yeah. Quint said you'd arrived. So was that a ghost or what?"

"I wouldn't care to swear. . . ."

"Come on, hon. You must have felt that cold. I come in here to get away from everybody, sort of old and cozy and, you know, classic. I'm sitting over there by the fireplace thinking about my motivation. The scenes we're shooting, you know? Quint is saving money by directing them himself, and he doesn't know diddley about motivation. Say, could we get out of this place?" Jazmin would have tossed flowing platinum tresses had her hair not been tastefully knotted into a French twist, the better to wear her little black hunting cap. She proceeded toward the door, still talking.

"Then I got to thinking about this maharani who was murdered, and these girls around the house talking about the ghosts. Ah . . ." The bright sun filled the entrance hall, along with the flowery, grassy scents of early summer. "So I start thinking about the spirits instead of motivation. You know, like the dead woman hasn't left us, she has more to say. And what do I see but this kind of shape in the chair, like glowing very faintly, and I felt the cold. I tell you, at first I was scared out of my scanties. Then I remembered what Chuck, my guru, says. He's from back home in Beverly Hills; that's in California. . . ."

Margaret nodded. Jazmin clearly would not stop until she had told her entire story. "Chuck says there are no boundaries between the spiritual world and this material world. You know, like channelers speak for these people who are still out there. You have channelers here? No? Never mind. So I calmed down and watched. I know I didn't imagine it. You came in, this thing shimmered and disappeared. I am like totally thrilled. We don't get stuff like this in Malibu."

"Indeed not," Margaret said. "I imagine murder is also comparatively rare."

"Wasn't that something, though? Right here in this house. Maniac on the loose, if you ask me." Jazmin did not seem terribly disturbed by the possibility.

"I doubt there's a maniac," Margaret said. "We are all presumably comparatively sane."

"If you say so," Jazmin said. "I only met most of them the other night."

"On the night of the murder, I understand you dined with my brother and some others," Margaret began.

"If you call it dining," Jazmin said. "I hate to complain, hon, but the food hasn't been all that great. I tried to persuade Quint to fly over some barbecue from this great place I know in Houston, or maybe some really good deli from the Stage in New York. He said the budget couldn't handle it. He is *so* cheap."

"I'm sorry about the food," Margaret said. "Mrs. Domby is usually more than adequate."

"I'd say there's trouble in the back of the house," Jazmin said. "I know from servants. Even that proper butler of yours would get the boot from me."

"Harbert? Whatever do you mean?"

"He was pretty rude to these Floods. Not that old Lester is any prize, and she is, in words of one syllable, unbelievable. Not my problem. You got to live next door to them. And the butler sure didn't have the time of day for Nigel. He's kind of cute, don't you think? I concentrated on the old maharajah. He's darling, in a foreign sort of way. He didn't actually eat with us, some kind of religious thing, he said, but La Belle Doris sure tucked it away. His wife, she says! The old dame that was murdered was his wife. Never mind; if you're as rich as he is, he can call Doris anything he wants."

When Jazmin finally paused for a breath, Margaret said, "I'm afraid our butler has a very strict view of who is worthy and who is not. My cousin Nigel is quite taken with you."

Jazmin's dazzling smile was entirely false. It seemed to say, "All men are taken with me. It's part of the job description."

"You know," Margaret said, "Nigel isn't any sort of a titled English gentleman, and never will be unless my brother dies without issue. A son, that is."

Jazmin shrugged. "Sure I know that. Still, he's fun. I'm never serious about men like Nigel. If you're interested in who's out to snag a title, you'd better keep an eye on that girlfriend of your brother's. If she married him, what would she be?"

"The Countess of Brayfield."

"Is that a fact? He'd be better off marrying me."

Margaret thought, please God, not that, and said aloud, "Why so? I haven't yet met Miss Waters."

"Let's just say that I wouldn't mind the occasional ghost showing up in the old ancestral home. Miss Manage-Things-My-Way-or-Else would cut the heart out of any ghost that got in her way. Trust me entirely on this." Then Jazmin smiled a lovely, luminous smile that Margaret knew could easily bring a strong man to his knees. "Don't worry, hon. Your brother is the last thing on my mind. If the dear old maharajah really has this stash of fabulous jewels to hand out, he's more my line. And now that he's a grieving widower . . ."

"With a spare wife," Margaret said.

Jazmin smiled. "Her jewels are really, really unimportant. You probably haven't seen her all got up, but I promise you I can see a flaw in a diamond from twenty feet."

"Before you take the plunge," Margaret said, "I'd advise you to ascertain the realities of quasi-royal life in an Indian desert palace."

"Oh, I know that," Jazmin said serenely. "You don't have to worry about me. Besides, you never really know about these foreigners, do you? He might have decided he could get rid of Wife Number One with no problem. I myself have a really strong sense of self-preservation." She moistened her lips to restore their gleam, and peered at her reflection in the glass covering the ancient document that gave the Priams title to the priory's lands.

"Indeed," Margaret said. "How foresighted of you."

"I'm just teasing about His Highness," Jazmin said with a merry little laugh. "He couldn't have done it."

"How would you know that?"

Jazmin fidgeted. She patted her hair and adjusted her red coat. "I just know, that's all. Well, I was planning to tell the man from the police, since I've talked it over with Quint. I mean, I don't want to get tied down here being a witness or anything like that."

Margaret waited, with a now calm Wally stretched out at her feet. Jazmin said finally, "The maharajah and I were having a lovely talk for a really long time after dinner that night. Just the two of us. After old Doris went off about her business, we were talking in one of these rooms, and then we went up in his tower. You know, the little room with stairs up from his suite upstairs?"

"I know," Margaret said. "I used to live here. You really

should inform the man from Scotland Yard immediately. It would perhaps eliminate the two of you as suspects."

Jazmin looked doubtful. "I couldn't *swear* to anything absolutely," she said finally. "I didn't have to say a word at this coroner's thing. I was . . . well, I did leave to go to my room for a few minutes to fix myself up a bit. Say, did you ever lie down on that god-awful bed? I've been sleeping on a pile of pillows and blankets on the floor. I didn't want to say anything, because the housekeeper seemed so pleased that some old queen or other had slept there."

Margaret skipped past the uncomfortable history of the bed in the Queen's Bedroom and forged ahead. "So you weren't together absolutely the whole time?"

Jazmin sighed. "Well, no. But the butler saw me. I went downstairs again to see if the brandy was still in that big room where we had drinks before dinner."

"Ah, the Great Hall, and Harbert saw you."

"He was clearing up, and he poured me a brandy. That's what butlers are for."

Margaret prodded a bit more. "Although you were with His Highness that evening, he was not yet a sad widower during the time you were together. Perhaps your attentions gave him a reason to want to free himself of encumbrances."

"Oh, no!" Jazmin said. "This wasn't, like, a sexual thing. It was just talk. I mean, sex is simple, don't you think? But talk is challenging. I'm always looking for challenges." She seemed quite proud of the fact.

"I wonder if Doris knows that."

"If it bothered her, hon, I'd be the one with a knife in my heart."

Chapter 9

Jazmin expressed a need to go off alone to think some more about motivation. Margaret thought that Jazmin's motivations were fairly obvious.

The hall where they had been conversing seemed to dim at the actress's departure, but it was merely the inevitable line of rain clouds moving across the sky. Margaret hoped that Quintus Roach was not depending too heavily on consistency in English weather.

Margaret set off to find her brother. She was still unnerved by the ghost of the gray lady, if that was what she had seen. A nice puzzling murder seemed positively ordinary by comparison, despite the number of unanswered questions: If the maharajah was in effect paying the Priory's bills via Roach, why would David try to dislodge him? Or could it be Doris whom David wanted to see removed? Or was Nigel's involvement complicating matters?

She came upon Harbert standing near the doors to the Great Hall. The fact that he was both idle and preoccupied did not escape her. She remembered Jazmin's opinion that there was turmoil behind the scenes.

She said boldly, "I understand you gave Miss Burns a brandy on the night of the murder."

Harbert frowned. "I attended to several of our guests," he said. "Miss Burns and the . . . Second Her Highness. I saw but did not speak to Mr. Roach as I was locking up. He was attempting to telephone to Los Angeles from the hall telephone.''

"I see," Margaret said. "Do you know where I might find my brother?"

Harbert turned and looked at her gravely. "He was about the grounds with Mr. Roach. I suggest the priory room or the walled garden. It's so difficult to tell where people are in all this confusion. . . . ''

"You horrible man, do not attempt to speak to me!"

Margaret and Harbert looked around as the sound of outraged upper-class England floated down the long hall. Then a definitively upper-class young Englishwoman strode toward them, followed by a nonplussed Quintus Roach. She had a Princess Di haircut, and wore resolutely flat shoes, a Laura Ashley flowered print skirt and a white blouse with lace collar, and a simple strand of pearls. She looked remarkably dowdy for someone so young, in spite of—or perhaps because of—her generous chest and ferocious scowl.

"I do not *perform!*" the young woman said loudly. "The very idea!"

Roach managed to get in a few more words: "But you can ride a horse, that's all I asked. You got a problem with that? A simple question?"

"Harbert, when is the next train to London?" The young woman, who Margaret surmised must be Chloe Waters, ignored everything except her snit.

"The next train is at three, Miss Waters," Harbert said soothingly. "However, Potts is planning to drive to London soon to fetch some supplies at Harrods for Mrs. Domby. Or perhaps Lady Margaret has a reason to drive to London."

Chloe was suddenly aware of Margaret and just as suddenly became utterly gracious. "Lady Margaret, I didn't realize it was *you*. Things have been so confused since the murder." She looked around to glare at Quintus Roach.

"A terrible thing," Margaret said. "What seems to be your problem, Mr. Roach?"

Chloe answered for him. "This person wants me to per-

form in a film. Wait, Harbert. I may still need to be driven
to the train.''

"I just wanted you in the polo scene," Roach said. He
turned toward Margaret to explain. "I need more riders. I
got these four extras, they cost a fortune, but it turns out polo
needs eight riders. I got the maharajah to agree to ride
around, and your brother said he'd do it. This Nigel Priam
who's turned up again says he'll do it. It's not like a real
game, just thundering hoofbeats, a lot of action, some fancy
editing.''

"What fun!" Margaret said cheerfully to spite Chloe's bad
temper. "Daddy had me up on a polo pony before I could
walk. I rather fancy joining in myself, so that's the four you
need. Miss Waters needn't perform. She can watch. She
won't be needing the car, Harbert. You may go." Harbert
went, on command.

"All *right*!" Roach said. "Let's do it! Be at the polo field
today about four for a kind of rehearsal so we can film tomorrow. I don't know if the maharajah will show up. He's
incommunicado." Roach said the word with relish. "That's
okay, as long as his bankers are still talking. Cheerio, kids."
He bustled away on his cinematic business.

Chloe said in a low, confiding voice, although there was
no one about to hear her, "Naturally I've been riding my
whole life, but we're more inclined to the hunt and point-
to-pointing than polo in my part of the world. It's just the
idea . . .''

"I'm sure David wouldn't want you to demean yourself by
acting in a film," Margaret said sweetly. "Although this film
is quite important to him." She did not need to add, "and
financially gratifying.''

"I *could* do it," Chloe said. She seemed to recognize the
value of pleasing David in view of her probable long-term
goals. "Although the murder has upset me terribly." Chloe
did not strike Margaret as a person who was deeply affected
by events that happened to people other than herself, however unpleasant.

"Very sad," Margaret said. "Did you know her well?"
"Who?"

"The maharani."

"Heavens, I can scarcely bring myself to speak to those people. I don't know that I ever saw her at all, and I've only caught glimpses of the others. At least they keep to themselves, and they mostly look the same, don't you think? Those saris, and jewels in their noses. I don't count that trollop Doris. I see far too much of her," she said contemptuously.

"Yet the murder has upset you?"

"It's the press. They're always trying to find scandalous things to say about our sort of people. They actually mentioned my name in one of their beastly papers. Daddy is terribly old-fashioned. A murder that involves a person like the maharajah and someone like David . . ." She wrinkled her nose. Not the kind of thing that happens to earls and others of high station. "I certainly don't like the idea of someone being able to break in. Security will have to be seen to around here." She spoke as though she would be outfitting the Priory personally in the very near future.

"It was not necessarily a break-in," Margaret said.

"Of course it was. Otherwise that would mean . . ." She stopped. A look of refined horror passed over her face. "If it were someone in this house, then it had to be one of the Indians, or Doris. Or that cousin of David's." She caught herself at the realization that Nigel was Margaret's cousin, too. "I mean, I understand that Nigel is quite the hell-raiser."

"He is that," Margaret said. "I suppose the police have spoken to you."

"I neither heard nor saw anything. I was up in David's rooms after dinner reading before I went off to my bed."

"Surely David wasn't reading." Margaret had no illusions about the range of her brother's intellectual pursuits. She wasn't watching Chloe as she spoke, but looked around quickly when there was no response.

"I was reading a lovely new novel, and he was about." Chloe was fingering her pearls nervously.

"About?"

"He nipped out once to find some papers downstairs in the estate office, but he was back in an instant."

Their eyes met, very briefly. "So as far as the police are

concerned, you were together." Margaret hoped that she had managed to conceal the rush of uneasiness she felt. This Sloane Ranger wench was providing a very poor alibi for David.

"Virtually so. At least until I went off to bed, very late," Chloe said. She, too, was uneasy. Like Margaret, she was perhaps wondering if David had some strange reason to murder one of his guests. If that was the case, poor Chloe would have to start over on her search for a suitable peer to wed.

"I wonder what route David took to the ground floor," Margaret said. She refused to believe that her brother was a murderer, but perhaps he had seen something that had been reported to Chloe.

Chloe hesitated again. "He never bothers with the main staircase," she said. "He takes those little stairs in his dressing room down to the pantry."

"I see," Margaret said, fully aware that the pantry led to the kitchen, and the kitchen had a door that led to the Nun's Walk and the walled garden. Fully aware as well that if David was off in the far reaches of the house on legitimate business in the estate office, Chloe herself could have made her way down to the Nun's Walk for a fateful encounter with the maharani. But the idea of this snobbish, spoiled young woman murdering an aging Indian lady was quite ridiculous. Her daddy would be *extremely* put out by such behavior. It isn't done.

"It's nearly time for lunch," Chloe said, relieved that there was an excuse to conclude this friendly chat.

"I shall pass on lunch," Margaret said. "See you on the polo field." She fled out the front door across the pebbled drive to the gate to the walled garden to look for her brother.

A wooden gate with an old-fashioned latch let her into the lush, tangled garden. Even under the gray, cloudy sky, the yard glowed with color. Pink climbing roses covered one wall, and sprays of blue lobelia dripped over the sides of squat stone urns. Purple and white irises grew at the edge of the shallow basin at the foot of the little fountain, and daisies and phlox and sweet peas bloomed in the borders. Mrs.

Domby had her own patch of herbs, where chives and mint, tarragon, chervil, and thyme were planted in neat rows.

David was sitting in an unpainted wicker chair, where the garden wall met the outside wall of his medieval hideaway. He was examining an accounts ledger.

"David, we've got to talk."

David looked up. Margaret thought he looked tired, but not especially guilty. On the other hand, guilt was not a strong family emotion, except with regard to cowardly acts. To wit, her avoidance of speaking directly to De Vere about her departure from New York. He would assume she was following some self-indulgent aristocratic whim, while she wished he were here to help her think through the problem of this murder. Westron seemed to be treading too carefully so as not to offend important personages. She didn't think the police were failing to pursue their leads, but De Vere would refuse to be awed by the pretensions of the upper classes, and would have had no reticence about demanding answers to reasonable questions. Alas, there was an ocean between them, even assuming that he still had any part in her life.

"What must we talk about?" David asked. He seemed to have forgotten that murder was afoot at Priam's Priory. He closed his accounts book. "Sit down, Margaret. Isn't the garden grand at this time of year? I much prefer this barely controlled jungle to what's left of the formal gardens."

David was taking the least stressful conversational route, so Margaret chose an easy subject for immediate discussion. "I met your lady friend just now. She'd gotten her knickers in a twist about 'performing' in Roach's film."

"Mmm." David gazed up at the sky, as if pondering whether the rain would hold off for a time or how his sister had given tongue to a less than elevated comment about Chloe.

Margaret persisted. "She seems to have . . . high aspirations."

"An *entirely* suitable match, dear boy, and time enough, I'd say. Your mother would have been so pleased." David mimicked a throaty upper-class grande dame voice. "That," he said, "is in effect the statement made by Chloe's mother not long ago." He grinned at last, and looked like the David Margaret liked best. "That ended the romance for me right there. I hate being pressured. However, I'd already invited Chloe to the Priory for the filming and to meet the maharajah, so here she is, but to depart as soon as possible."

"Is she aware of the change in her status? I think not," Margaret said, but she was nevertheless relieved that Chloe was not a leading contender to become Countess of Brayfield. "Now let us talk about Doris."

David became greatly interested in the dark green binding of his accounts ledger. "Doris isn't a bad sort," he said finally. "You'll see when you meet her."

"We've met," Margaret said. "She invaded my room this morning, talking rubbish about the ghosts disliking her, and her hard life with Highness in India." She added reluctantly, "And about knowing you and Nigel in London. Explain that, will you?"

"What did she tell you?"

"No good, David. A question answered by a question is not acceptable. You tell me."

David thought a minute and said, "She's a girl from the country, rather good-looking in a different sort of way, don't you think? She ran away from some sticky situation in her home village and came to London. I had that flat in Chelsea, where Nigel popped in to stay from time to time. One day he brought Doris. He was playing at Pygmalion, fixing up her looks and her accent to help her along in London. She learned fast. I went about with her a bit. Good fun, not nearly so almighty regal as she's become since she hooked up with Ram-Sam."

"I'm given to understand that you arranged the hook-up."

He shrugged. "I helped her find a job at his London bank. They met. They hit it off."

"I'd like someone to explain *that*," Margaret said. "Not a likely pair. I would have guessed that His Highness would prefer someone with a bit more flash."

"Like Jazmin," David said.

"Exactly," Margaret said. "In fact, Miss Burns has indicated that she has established the . . . foundations of a relationship with him. To wit, sitting late with him on the night of the murder.'' A tiny frown appeared on David's fair brow. Margaret went on carefully. ''Just as you and Chloe were sitting late in your rooms, conveniently supplying a mutual alibi for the approximate time of the murder, although not a perfect one.''

''Chloe insisted upon staying in my sitting room for a time. She's definitely *not* staying in my rooms, if that's what you're asking. And what do you mean, 'not perfect'? I don't need an alibi.''

''Someone stabbed the maharani. I understand that the police like to know where people were when a crime occurred. Chloe said that you took yourself off to the estate offices sometime after dinner, by way of the stairs that lead readily to the Nun's Walk.''

''Surely you don't think that I . . .'' David stood up and paced back and forth on the circle of gray flagstones on which the wicker garden chairs rested. ''Why would I wish ill of the maharani?''

''Or Doris, for whom the dead lady might easily have been mistaken. Doris herself suggested that the maharani in her sari in the dark of night might have been murdered in error, that Doris was the intended victim.''

''Doris has always been full of fantasies,'' David said. ''I have convinced Westron that I had nothing to do with the murder.'' He looked straight at her. Unless she could no longer read her brother, she was sure he was telling the truth.

''Then what of Nigel?''

David looked glum. ''Nigel poses a problem, doesn't he? He said he went right off to London after dinner, but did he? He has plenty of friends in the neighborhood from the old days where he could have dossed down. He indicated that he had some business in these parts other than visiting the old family estate.'' David shrugged unconvincingly.

''Might he have returned here that night, murdered the maharani for no good reason other than to steal her jewels?'' Margaret hated to hear herself speak the words. Nigel was, after all, a Priam. "That's rather far-fetched, even for a man with few recognizable limits."

"I will not consider the possibility," David said. He plucked a full-blown rose from the climbing bush. A shower of pinkish petals fell at his feet.

"Then what about the maharajah? We only know him as Daddy's chum from the old days, an exotic creature who spoiled us as children and imposes on us as adults. Could he have decided that he could conveniently remove his wife, leaving him free—freer—to regularize his relationship with Doris? Or begin something new with this Jazmin?"

"Jazmin is deeply interested in her film career," David said, "and all that pertains to it." He had a momentary look of longing. Margaret was beginning to suspect that Jazmin Burns had captured the fancy of all the sentient men in the vicinity, with the possible exceptions of Harbert and Potts, and of them she could not be certain. "I suppose Doris also told you that the maharajah is financing part of Roach's film," he said. "Thereby helping to subsidize the Priory for a few more months. That's one reason I haven't simply tossed him out. These are difficult times."

"The sale of Rime Manor to the Floods helped greatly with your finances, certainly. How did you ever find them? And more important, convince them to pay good money for the place?"

David looked uncomfortable. "Actually, Nigel brought them around. Part of his business hereabouts. For a modest consideration, naturally."

"He asked a commission from you." She sighed. "Nigel surely didn't tell the Floods what a wretched condition the place was in."

"I believe he emphasized its charms and historical importance, and not the cost of restoration. The Flood fellow is quite sharp. He must have seen at once that it needed work, but the wife was terribly keen. Did you know he made a fortune in construction, creating little towns and shopping centers in the middle of those endless wheat fields they have over in America? He and I may be doing further business, if this murder doesn't ruin everything."

"Oh?"

"Nothing definite," David said quickly. "It's only talk now. But if Highness were to be driven away by danger and scandal, taking his money with him so that Roach has to withdraw from the filming, I should be in a pretty bad financial state. An arrangement with Flood could save the day."

"Arrangement?"

"A megadevelopment project," David said. "That's what he calls it. It would allow our ghosts to roam in peace for our lifetimes at least."

She found the prospect of a "mega" anything appalling, but she didn't care to dampen his enthusiasm just now. Instead she said, "About our ghosts. I'm sure the gray lady was lurking about the music room just now. I felt that strange cold people talk about. Poor Wally very nearly collapsed from terror. Jazmin claims she saw the ghost clearly. She's thrilled. She can dine out on her tale all over Beverly Hills."

"Write it down in the book, will you?" David said. The Priams had kept a book of ghostly sightings for a hundred years. "The paranormal people love records of sightings," he said with a grin. "I was thinking of having a little book printed about all of them, and sell it to the sightseers for several guineas. I wish I could sell off one of the ghosts as easily as I did the Manor. Mrs. Flood would 'adore' having a ghost."

Suddenly David came out of his gloom. "It'll be all right. Her Highness's death was an accident. We're all civilized people here, except possibly Roach. I do want everything cleared up soon. I have center court tickets for Wimbledon."

Chapter 10

"*Luncheon, your* lordship." Harbert had made his way silently through the garden, with old Wally huffing at his heels. Margaret wondered if Harbert had been lurking behind the gooseberry bush to listen in on brother and sister in conference, so suddenly had he appeared.

"I shall not be lunching here," Margaret said. "I have business in the village. David, Nigel needs a talking to. I'll have a chat with him when we've had this polo rehearsal."

Harbert cleared his throat. "Lord Brayfield, forgive me for mentioning it, but is it wise to have Mr. Nigel in residence? He seems to be attracting his many friends from the London press. They upset the staff. I have had to turn away half a dozen this morning alone. And the maids are whispering that Mr. Nigel could be the murderer. Nothing Mrs. Domby says can stop the gossip."

"That will be all, Harbert," David said firmly. "Nigel remains."

"Very good, sir," Harbert said. His disapproval was total. He led them from the garden. Wally made a feeble attempt to frolic at Margaret's heels. "We cannot take the Nun's Walk to reach the dining room," Harbert said. "The police continue to block it off."

As they passed the entrance to the Nun's Walk, Margaret saw an official-looking seal on the door.

The little parade made its way to the front of the house. Once inside, Harbert and David proceeded down the hallway and turned near the screens passage at the end of the Great Hall. Margaret took the main staircase up to her room. At the top of the stairs, she paused. A few steps to her left would take her to the door of the maharajah's suite. If she knocked and was admitted, she could request an immediate interview, and state that the maharajah should then and there speak openly to the police.

She did not knock. If her appointment later was not kept, she might have a chance to speak on the polo field. If he failed to appear there, she would then storm the suite and see him.

The scent of incense and Indian spices was especially heavy, but the halls were silent and empty. She turned right and walked past David's rooms, then down the hall toward her own. As she passed the bedroom next to David's, she heart Quintus Roach's voice, speaking rather loudly. Of course he would be placed in the second best of the guest rooms, next to the Queen's Bedroom, which had been commandeered by Jazmin. He might easily be venting his annoyance about his own dreadfully uncomfortable albeit historically significant bed.

"Dammit, Jazzie!" Roach's voice was very clear. "You're not going to screw up the deal on this movie. You can't take off with that man. You don't know anything about him."

Margaret could not hear Jazmin's reply, but she heard that merry laugh again behind the closed door.

Roach spoke again, "I don't care how many diamonds he has in his turban; at least you got to stick around for the scenes here. Otherwise all these chumps will pull out, and my money guys in the States are counting on you."

As Margaret was letting herself into her room to fetch her handbag, Jazmin emerged from Roach's room.

"You got a contract," Roach shouted after her, "and I'll hold you to it."

"So sue me," Jazmin said over her shoulder. "Or pay me. If you can get the suckers to pay you." She caught sight of Margaret and waved. "Seen any more ghosts?"

Margaret shook her head.

"Me neither, but I'm looking all the time. And I'm starved," Jazmin said. "It's this fabulous country air."

Margaret watched the other woman's shapely red-coated figure undulate toward the main staircase, her sleek thighs encased in silvery beige spandex riding breeches. Amazing. Then she gathered her handbag from her room and went downstairs to find where Potts had parked her car.

Out on the drive, the bearded young man she had seen earlier was squinting at a large piece of equipment whose purpose Margaret did not know, but which was presumably required to record the dramatic polo scenes to come. Margaret was beginning to feel somewhat apprehensive about attempting a challenging sport which she had only toyed with, and certainly hadn't practiced in years. Except for that weekend in Palm Beach when the handsome ten-goal Argentinian player had suggested she join in a practice.

"I beg your pardon," Margaret said to the young man. "As you seem to be involved in the filming, I wonder if you know exactly what is expected of us."

"Us?" The young man looked her over, as though trying to place her as a film actress he might recognize.

"Mr. Roach has asked me and my brother and some others to ride as part of the polo scenes. I've been thinking that since none of us are professionals, it seemed odd that he would simply toss us into an expensive film."

"Odd." The young man was given to one-word responses. He fiddled with the light meter slung around his neck.

"Definitely odd," Margaret said. "One assumes that he is cutting corners. Financially, that is."

"Hah." He continued to examine her. Then he squinted up into the sky, now entirely covered with gray clouds. The rain would come soon. Finally he decided to speak a sentence. "If he's hired me as his director of photography for this so-called film epic, he is cutting corners. Yes."

"I don't understand."

The young man scratched his nose, looked at his light meter, nudged a cable with his toe. "Not that I'm not glad of the chance,'' he said. ''The film business isn't terrific here in the old UK, so you take what you can get, even if you're not technically qualified, and the conditions are less than ideal.''

''Am I to understand that Mr. Roach is expending little money on this production, in spite of his grand plans?''

''Exactly, love,'' the young man said. ''I come cheap. And I operate the camera and act as my own assistant and loader. He's got an electrician and a fellow to do heavy work with the crane and laying tracks. He's picked up a lady who's got together some costumes and does a bit of hair and makeup. He even hired some people to ride. It's quite the joke amongst us. But if I get a credit—if the film does get made, start to finish—it'll be useful. We've been betting that most of the budget is going toward paying the dolly with the platinum hair.''

''I see,'' Margaret said.

''Likely you don't see at all,'' he said. ''It's some kind of scam; haven't figured out what. He did find me an old Arriflex that ought to be in a museum. There's some kind of Steadicam I'm supposed to use, but I can manage that. I couldn't tell you what kind of film stock he's managed to get. Bits of this and that, I'd guess, so I actually film something. All I know is he told me to get as much as I could on film and do it with natural light, except for the close-ups of this Jazmin Burns. We got lights for her.'' Quintus Roach's director of photography shrugged. ''I shot a couple of documentaries of student riots and Pakistanis milling around protesting. I guess I can film a few horses running wild.''

''And I guess I can ride one of them.''

''Where'd he find you to hire?''

''Right out of the fields, as it were,'' Margaret said.

''Well then. You're working cheap, too. No union to worry you, and if you get a few still photos out of it, like you were in a real film, you've got something to put in your portfolio.''

''There you have it,'' Margaret said. ''I say, are you living in those caravans down in the park?''

''Beastly, they are. The loos smell something terrible.''

''Come round for drinks here this evening at the house,''

Margaret said. He looked doubtful. "I have certain privi-leges, being on the acting side of this venture. I didn't hear your name."

"Geoff," he said. "I couldn't come without my mates, but that's only three others."

"You must all come, by all means," Margaret said. "And I'll be seeing you on the polo field this afternoon for our rehearsal."

"If the bloody rain holds off. You know how big that field is?"

"Ten acres," Margaret said. "Horses need a lot of room."

"I'm surprised the coppers are letting us get on with it, what with this murder they're talking about. Our crew got here day after it happened," Geoff said, "so we heard all the gossip. You'd think the place would be in a uproar, but it's business as usual."

"Show business," Margaret said. "No business like it." She had a momentary vision of millions of pounds sterling contributed by the maharajah and the Floods—with a com-mission to Nigel—disappearing into Quintus Roach's pock-ets, while poor David merely hoped to keep the Priory living on into the twenty-first century.

"What do you make of this?" Geoff fiddled with a nylon backpack resting on a pile of cables. "I found it tossed in among the cabling just now. It looks valuable."

He presented Margaret with a remarkable sight: a dagger eight inches long with a curved white hilt of ivory inlaid with colored stones. The double-edged blade looked exceedingly sharp. Margaret had seen something similar, sheathed in a velvet scabbard, among the Eastern antiques sold by her old employer Bedros Kasparian in his Madison Avenue shop. A weapon of an era in Indian history when Mogul emperors lived in Delhi and brought great parts of the subcontinent under their sway. She did not remember seeing anything like it in the various collections at Priam's Priory.

"Have a look," Geoff said, and handed over the dagger carelessly. "There's a stone or two missing. I was wondering if the Indian fellow tossed it away. I hear he's so rich, he probably wouldn't care to have a damaged piece about."

"It was his wife who was stabbed," Margaret said. She took the dagger carefully between two fingers, knowing there probably wouldn't be any fingerprints, if people still tracked down that kind of thing. But if it had been used to murder Her Highness, there might still be some evidence attached to it. She looked at it more closely, and she was sure that those were diamonds and rubies that formed the petals of the flower motif on the hilt, with emeralds for the leaves.

"Please take this into the house at once," Margaret said, "and ask the butler to take you to Mr. Westron from Scotland Yard. Explain to him how you came to find it, and why you didn't report your discovery immediately."

"But I did. I mean, I just found it a bit before you came around. It couldn't have been there more than a day, since we just brought the equipment up here yesterday. It wasn't lying on the ground then or anything. We would have seen it."

"Tossed in well after the murder then," Margaret said, half to herself. "Go along and tell the inspector the exact truth."

Geoff nodded doubtfully. Margaret continued to look at him until he shrugged and headed toward the front door. Margaret's doubts that he would present the evidence as she requested were erased by the appearance of Westron at the door, ready to depart for his own lunch somewhere other than Priam's Priory. Geoff looked over his shoulder at Margaret, and she nodded encouragement.

Westron listened to Geoff's tale with his head cocked, reached out and took the dagger. Then he gestured to indicate that Geoff should precede him into the house.

Margaret wondered if by forcing Geoff to hand over the knife, she had started a sequence of events that would bring trouble to the dear old maharajah. She looked up. The windows of the maharajah's suite were directly above the jumble of movie equipment. She looked farther up, toward the chimneys and roofs. Nigel was staying on the very top floor. She wondered if Uncle Lawrence had that sort of rare Mogul dagger among his collected memories of India.

Potts came around the corner of the house with a bucket and a spade, bent on an outdoor task. She stopped him.

"Potts, please go around and tell Mrs. Domby that I've invited some people around for drinks tonight about seven. Not for dinner."

Potts looked momentarily confused. Messages of this sort were not his usual task.

"I have to be on my way," Margaret said, "and I don't have the time to tell her myself."

"I'll do it, m'lady." Potts scratched his head and plotted his course. "Mr. Harbert will want to know, too. He gets mighty annoyed if he doesn't know what's going on. I seen him tear into the maids and outside boys something fierce. Not that he'd dare such with me, but he has a temper, that one."

"I'm sure he's just doing his job as he sees it. Oh, Potts," Margaret said. "Do you still rake the drive here every day?"

"I do," he said, "every morning. Except today. I'd just finished up yesterday when they moved this movie business in, so I told his lordship I wouldn't be doing it again until they shoved off. No reason for doing pointless work, I say. He agreed."

"Quite right," Margaret said. As she headed for her car, Potts was on his way to the kitchen side to convey the message to Mrs. Domby.

A light rain finally started to fall as Margaret drove through the Priory's parkland toward Upper Rime. A hopeful break in the clouds to the southwest promised a bit of sun later in the afternoon. The black and white cows in the meadows had clustered together in a patient group to await the end of the rain. Or perhaps they were enjoying the shower. Margaret had never been able to read the thoughts of large purebred bovines, although she got on well with horses.

That set her thinking about what sort of animals Roach intended his cinematic polo players to ride. Polo ponies had a high degree of training and if he thought to use any of her father's surviving ponies, they would be terribly out of training.

She hoped for the best. A headlong gallop—or as best as

could be coaxed from an aged pony—couldn't be too demanding. She tried to recall all her lessons on holding the mallet and rising up from the saddle to strike the tiny white ball in the midst of the vast polo field. She felt a thrill of anticipation at the idea of riding with the maharajah—even if it was possibly an empty gesture that in the end would only profit Quintus Roach.

Chapter 11

The narrow streets of Upper Rime were empty in the midday rain, which was darkening the pale limestone of the crooked old buildings. Margaret parked at the edge of the village green and dashed through the rain to the welcome snugness of the Riming Man Pub. The few tourists who managed to reach Upper Rime invariably labeled the pub "quaint" because of its close-studded uprights of dark wood and whitewashed panels. It had been quainter still in the days when it still had a thatched roof, but the expense of upkeep and the difficulty in finding thatchers in the modern world had forced a replacement with tiles.

The painted sign over the door, with a figure of a troubadour and his lute, suggested a history going back to the Middle Ages, but it was a nineteenth-century building that consciously reproduced and romanticized the distant past.

A few farmers had come in from their work for a midday pint, and a couple of men who looked as though they might be involved in setting up the rides and booths for the coming fair had ducked in from the rain.

"Well, Lady Margaret, we've been hearing that you're home." The man behind the bar was Margaret's contemporary, known during his teenage years as Terrible Ted, the preeminent village bad boy. Indeed, Nigel on his annual summer visits to Priam's Priory (for the improving influence of his aunt the countess) had shared a certain number of disgraceful escapades with Ted. The years had mellowed Ted from teen terrorist to reasonably respectable businessman.

"You'll like a half of Ruttles, if I remember," Ted said. He raised his voice. "Lys, bring a half for Lady Margaret."

Margaret saw at the end of the long bar a slim, sultry-eyed girl with thick, dark hair, wearing a denim work shirt and jeans.

"Remember me little sis?" Ted said. "Alice she was, calls herself Lys now. Been up to Oxford, and down again with a lot o' learning. Been helping about the pub until she goes off to some fancy job in London in September. Wants no part of the country, or the lads hereabouts. She's had a dozen marriage offers since she's been back."

Lys put a foaming glass on the bar in front of Margaret.

"Hullo," Margaret said. "I remember you as a child."

Lys smiled. She was a very pretty young woman. "Your brother was in. He said you'd be here from America."

"The place is full of nobs today," Ted said with a grin, and indicated with his chin a couple sitting alone in a dim corner. "Poor dears can't even light a fire in the dump they bought, so they come in for a bite of bread and cheese near every day."

Phyllis and Lester Flood wore fixed smiles as they ex-changed sporadic sentences, scarcely to be defined as a con-versation. The locals gave them a wide berth. Both wore tweeds, which were fine for the country when the cold winds arrived, but not for the summer season that was full upon the land.

"They've never bought a round for the pub," Lys said, "so people tend to ignore them. I wanted to tell them, but Ted said let them find their own way." Lys went off to serve a lanky youth whose gaze indicated that he was deeply smit-ten by her.

"I shall have a word with the Floods," Margaret said. "They know my brother, and we have mutual acquaintances in New York. Ted, you've heard all about the troubles at the Priory?"

He nodded, but offered no comment. He polished the bar with a cloth, even though the dark wood was spotless.

Margaret kept trying. "I suppose the police have asked you if there are rumors of some local lad doing a break-in and getting into more than he bargained for." Although she was certain that the break-in story could not be sustained, she hoped that she would discover it was true.

Ted pointedly began to busy himself polishing glasses, quite unnecessarily. Then he said, "No such rumors about." He looked at her. "I wouldn't put the coppers onto any friend of mine."

"Not Nigel, I don't mean Nigel," Margaret said quickly. "I meant the younger boys in the village."

Ted warmed, but only a bit. "Nothing like that being talked about. I would have heard. We've got a few rough lads, rougher than Nigel and me were in the old days. We were talking about that just this morning, all this drug business and violence that's around. He came up from London last evening on the late train and stayed the night here. The constable took him off to the big house this morning. I suppose you know that. Lady Margaret, he's done nothing. I know old Nigel."

"I hope you're right," Margaret said. "Thanks. Let me speak to the Floods. They look dreadfully unhappy."

"So would you," Ted said cheerfully, "if you was pouring a fortune into that wreck of a house. Village should have made your brother tear it down years ago, history or no."

Margaret left him to serve a customer. "Hullo," she said to the Floods. "We've met in Manhattan. Margaret Priam. You know my brother."

Lester and Phyllis looked up, pathetically glad to hear a friendly voice. Phyllis was fighting off middle age to the best of her ability, with hair artfully highlighted with gold. The rings on her fingers were better suited to Fifth Avenue than the High Street of an English village, and she did look wilted in her tweeds. She had not, however, succumbed to sensible country brogues, but wore dainty high-heeled pumps with open toes.

"Lady Margaret. Of course," Phyllis said. "What a surprise. To see you in this place, I mean. Dear David mentioned that you were flying over.''

"Except for the village fair twice a year and the cinema in the next town," Margaret said, "the Riming Man is our only excuse for regular entertainment.''

The farmers finished their pints and headed back to their labors. There was a murmur of greetings as they passed Margaret, not overly cordial, not noticeably hostile. Most of the people in the village and the surrounding farms had known Margaret since she was a child. Most of them had grudgingly approved of her late father, but many probably failed to appreciate her brother. Many were no doubt gleeful about the troubles at the Priory.

"It must seem like a very simple life compared to New York and . . .'' Margaret couldn't remember what midwestern American metropolis had produced the Floods.

"Simple!" Phyllis Flood had the sound of a woman who had gone far, far beyond the end of her tether. "You cannot imagine what I've been through since Lester took it into his head to buy Rime Manor. Where was it you hooked up with Nigel Priam, Lester? Some gambling club or other in London.''

"Hush, Phyl. Lady Margaret doesn't want to hear about our troubles. She's got plenty of her own.''

"Well, it is distressing," Margaret began, and yearned to find out exactly how Nigel had discovered the Floods and what he had promised them.

"I should say so," Lester said. "They don't hang people here anymore, I understand, but if my brother was in as deep as yours . . .''

"David is not deep into anything," she said with conviction. She was reminded of why the Floods had not been popular in New York.

"Way I figure it," Lester said, "he's got his money problems, and he's got those women after him. Cold-blooded wench, that Chloe Waters is; then there's Doris, the phony maharani. And Miss Jazmin Burns, who told me herself that she'd like to retire from the movies and marry a title.''

"Not without a lot of money, I'm sure," Margaret said,

"which my brother doesn't happen to have. And what would that have to do with murdering the maharani?"

"I'd say it was Doris in her Indian getup the fellow thought he was murdering. Not that I'm saying it was your brother. But I told the police there was bad feeling about her all around. Jazmin even said so." He seemed extraordinarily pleased to be on a first-name basis with a Big Star. "I had to tell the police what I thought."

You didn't, not really, Margaret thought, but said, "Naturally one must assist the police whenever possible."

"I told Lester it was none of his damned business," Phyllis said, "and if Lord Brayfield gets hauled off to jail, there's no way I'd spend another minute at Rime Manor. He's the only thing approaching civilization for miles. I don't think one person has spoken to us of their own accord since we got here three weeks ago."

"It takes time to be accepted in small villages like Upper Rime," Margaret said. "I don't imagine even our butler, who's been here for five or six years, is thought of as anything but a foreigner, and he's from somewhere nearby."

"Don't I know the feeling," Phyllis said. "People are much friendlier back in Ohio. We never should have come here. Even New York wasn't this bad."

"Now, Phyllis, you were the one who wanted to pull up roots and go to Manhattan," Lester said. "I paid a fortune for that apartment on Fifth Avenue, Lady Margaret, and another fortune to have it decorated, and *then* we find out it isn't in one of the right buildings, and that obnoxious person with his fabrics and paints wasn't one of the right decorators." He poured out old grievances with a vengeance, the better to forget his new ones. "We'd get these invitations to dinners and galas and end up shelling out a couple of thousand bucks for some charity I'd never heard of to stand around with a bunch of people who looked right through us."

"It wasn't me who decided to buy that ruin," Phyllis said. "I tell you, Lady Margaret, we've got horrible problems. We managed to find a man in London who's quite an expert on restoring old buildings, but he costs the earth, and progress is very, very slow. Lester knows everything about construction, but he can't make heads or tails of what they're up to."

"Nothing like building a shopping mall, I expect. I hope to have a look at your house sometime," Margaret said politely.

"Maybe you could give us some advice," Phyllis said eagerly. You English always know just what's right for these old places."

"I'm afraid I know nothing of restoring old buildings," Margaret said. "And I do have to get back to the Priory." She was suddenly aware that Ted was hovering behind her chair.

He leaned down and whispered in her ear, "The press. You'd better hop it. One of them may have recognized you. Take the back door out." Ted picked up the empty glasses on the Floods' table and returned to his post behind the bar.

A cluster of damp men demanded attention at the bar. They were certainly not locals. Lys served the drinks and chatted them up animatedly. She caught Margaret's eye, and nodded toward the back door, as if to say, "Get along while I distract them."

"Perhaps I do have a bit of time before I have to be back," Margaret said to the Floods. "Shall we go along now? I'll just get my car and meet you at the Manor." She departed so quickly by the back door that the Floods had no time to discuss the matter.

As Margaret drove along the narrow lanes to Rime Manor, she was relieved to see that only the Floods in a deep maroon Jaguar sedan followed her. Not the best auto for country life, but at least they hadn't succumbed to a Rolls or a Daimler.

Rime Manor was set in the midst of a raggedy lawn, with a rather charming pond before it and a few old trees behind it. The lawn would need some expensive care to revive it, and the house itself had a weary, derelict look. On the scaffolding erected around the gray limestone walls, a lone workman high up near the roof was picking away at a crooked window frame with a tool while another contemplated this activity from below with folded arms. A grubby boy was mixing cement unenthusiastically in a small trough. Stacks of roofing tiles were piled near the door.

The Jaguar screeched to a stop close on her heels.

"I remember creeping up on the house when I was a child. It had long been abandoned by then," Margaret said. "Very historical," she added quickly, "but no one in these parts could afford to keep it up. The first house was the farmhouse for the old priory, and this one was built in the eighteenth century. Quite a treasure."

"No ghosts, though," Phyllis said crossly.

"Hell, Phyllis, you don't need a ghost. You need a fellow who can hammer nails, or what are those things called? Mortise joints? I can't follow what the restoration guy is talking about. Cruck and wychert and cob. Daub and wattle. Galleting." Lester was growing grumpy. "All I want is a nice room to sit in, and a place to put my guns and fishing gear. Some pheasants to shoot and a trout in the stream. That's what I want."

"Hot and cold running water, a decent shower, a freezer, ice cubes in my drink. A ceiling that doesn't drop bits of bat do in my hair." Phyllis was beginning to whine. "I wanted a house like Priam's Priory."

Lester reached out and patted Phyllis's hand. Someday, Margaret thought, if the restoration of Rime Manor didn't bankrupt him, Lester Flood would surely find Phyllis a house just like Priam's Priory—if not the Priory itself.

"You'll be able to have a lovely garden," Margaret said as she followed them to the house. "And I see you have ducks." A mother duck paddled across the pond with four fluffy ducklings behind her.

"Greedy wretches," Phyllis said. "They hang out at the back door and scream to be fed. Worse than those freeloaders we used to meet at parties in New York."

"I should have built from the ground up," Lester said as he opened the door to the women. "That's the business I know. Forget this historical stuff. I suppose your brother has told you that I'd be willing to take some of his land off his hands. If I had the right acreage, I could let this place go to hell, build a nice place for Phyl and me, and then put up a few houses for these London fellows who want a country place.''

Margaret winced at the thought of London barristers and stockbrokers as near neighbors, crowding the narrow lanes with their Range Rovers and Volvo estate cars, all thanks to Lester Flood. She hoped it would never come to that. The disruption would take a long time to be accepted by the locals.

Lester stood back to allow Margaret a glimpse of the ground floor. She had no clear memory of the interior of Rime Manor, since throughout her childhood it was abandoned, and was therefore deemed too dangerous for exploration. Now she saw that by dint of a good deal of work and much money, it could be made livable. The proportions were distinguished, and the old wood paneling was still in place on the walls. Someone had been at work stripping it down. Phyllis had managed to truck in some fairly decent and rather expensive furniture for half of the principal drawing room, so that corner of the house was habitable.

''Charming,'' Margaret said.

''Her Highness thought so,'' Phyllis said, as she slipped off her high-heeled shoes and padded about in her stockinged feet. ''At least, she said, 'Lovely, very lovely' more than once.''

''Indeed? Which highness would that be?'' It was hard to imagine Doris condescending to pay a call on the Floods.

''The late maharani,'' Phyllis said. ''I met her when they first arrived quite by chance, while I was walking about the Priory grounds, near the quaint little house by the lake. Then she sent word that she'd like to visit, and she came to call only a day or two before she was murdered. Your Mr. Harbert drove her here with one of her ladies. I guess she was pretty bored at the Priory. I sent Lester away for the afternoon, as I was given to understand that Indian ladies do not socialize with men.''

''That is true of some old-fashioned Eastern ladies,'' Margaret said. ''Whatever did you talk about?'' She could not imagine what such two different women had to say to one another.

"The usual things. She had worries about her husband," Phyllis said. "But don't we all? Lester's cholesterol is much too high, but he insists on eating these big English breakfasts with eggs and sausages. I think she found out something about Doris. You know how women look when they find out dirt about the Other Woman? Half-pleased, half-crazy waiting for the moment of revenge."

Margaret couldn't help but notice that Lester started to hum uneasily. He edged away to inspect a not very distinguished painting of dead animals hanging on one wall. Poor old Lester probably had a guilty secret or two of his own.

"Did she speak of actual danger to him?"

Phyllis frowned. "Not in so many words. She disliked England and wanted to return home to India. She implied she'd found a reason to convince him to depart. Personally, I think that Doris was having a fling with someone, and when the maharani told the maharajah, he'd boot Doris out and head for the hills of home."

"Who?" Margaret could not imagine her brother or Nigel—or even Roach—engaging in a "fling" with Second Her Highness.

"She didn't say," Phyllis said.

"The old prince liked the looks of Jazmin," Lester said. "I wonder if the old wife knew about that. Doris sure did. You noticed that yourself, Phyl, when we were at the Priory for dinner the night the wife was killed."

"I noticed that the Priory isn't damp, they have servants who treat you right, and mice don't have conventions in the middle of the living room floor. And I noticed that you liked Jazmin Burns's looks, too." Phyllis was becoming shrill again. She turned to Margaret. "Is it too much to ask for a working furnace and floors that are a few centuries younger than my grandfather?"

"These old floors will be lovely with a little work," Margaret said. "I say, Phyllis, shall we run down to London while I'm here? I love to visit the shops around Regent Street and Knightsbridge."

"That would be fun," Phyllis said. There was a brightness

in her eyes that seemed to indicate that Margaret had awoken the part of her psyche dedicated to shopping. "I could pick up a few more things for the house, if they can manage to fix the roof tiles so it doesn't leak. And maybe some new clothes. This Harvey Nichols is supposed to be good. Chloe Waters mentioned it. She said that Beauchamp Place has lots of lovely shops."

"We can stop at Harrods," Margaret said. "It's similar to Bloomingdale's, only better. Mr. Flood, I'll have Potts come round tomorrow to have a word with the people who are working on your renovation. He probably knows them all. He can express the Earl of Brayfield's interest in having the place shaped up rather more quickly than at the current pace."

"That would be more than a gift," Lester said. "I'd owe you one."

"Rather than owing me anything," Margaret said, "you might make a contribution to whatever cause the fair this weekend is in honor of. Word of a generous gesture gets about rather quickly in a village of this size. The vicar is probably trying to raise money to restore falling beams in the village church."

"Lady Margaret, I am becoming an expert in the costs of restoration." Lester seemed about to whip out a checkbook to buy his way into the good graces of the residents of Upper Rime.

"Excellent," Margaret said. "And buy a round for the locals the next time you're at the pub. They expect that sort of thing. We'll have this place in good shape in no time, and the vicar will be as happy as a sandboy with an extra hundred pounds from you. Now I do have to be getting back to the Priory. Mr. Roach expects me to ride in his preposterous polo scene. We're rehearsing this afternoon. David and Nigel and perhaps even the maharajah."

"We expect to be there," Phyllis said. "Lester likes to keep an eye on how his money is being spent."

"Ah. So you have also invested in Mr. Roach's film," Margaret said. She was becoming exceedingly impressed by Quintus Roach's ability to extract money from the unwary.

"A bit," Lester said. "He needed a little extra financing for something that had gone over budget. I didn't get all the technical details, but he's given me profit participation. Points. Way I figure it, movies are the one thing that's making money these days. Look at the Japanese. They know what's what, and they're buying up Hollywood."

"So true," Margaret said. "You'll stay for drinks."

Phyllis beamed. This was more like gracious country living. "Just so's there are no more murders," she said gaily. "We lock this place up tight as a drum now. I said those very words to your Mr. Harbert. Such a gentleman."

Margaret raised an eyebrow.

"I hope we can find someone just like him for this place." Phyllis spoke so offhandedly that Margaret looked at her closely. Yes, Phyllis Flood was toying seriously with the idea of poaching the Priory's butler. She ought to suggest to David that he give Harbert a rise in wages.

"You'll find someone," Margaret said. "They have wonderful agencies that find all sorts of servants." But now she was thinking again about the secret the maharani had discovered that would convince her husband to leave England. She'd never had the chance to tell him, because someone who also knew the reason had silenced her. That person was in or about the Priory.

"Not to worry about murders," she said as she took her leave of Phyllis and Lester, and kicked her way through a flock of noisy ducks. "Murder really is quite rare around here."

Chapter 12

Margaret drove slowly back to Priam's Priory. As she passed the gates into the drive, she saw Westron gazing up at the front of the house. He came over to her as she got out of her car.

"Lady Margaret, Mr. Roach has told me that he met you previously in the United States, in Los Angeles. Does this signify that you know something of the film business?"

"It does not," Margaret said. "Alas, or thank goodness."

Westron was disappointed. "I was hoping you'd know something of his background."

Margaret smiled. "I am certain that what Mr. Roach knows best is how to attract funding. I cannot speak for what he knows about making movies beyond that. Geoff told me—"

"The lad who brought me the knife." Westron nodded. "Hired on the cheap in London, along with a minimum crew of novices with little real experience. Somehow this Roach got around our unions. Going through the motions is how I see it. What do you make of it?"

She thought a minute and said, "I make of it that Quintus Roach is collecting a substantial sum from investors—the maharajah, Lester Flood, and probably others who have been enticed by the glamour of films, as represented in the flesh by Jazmin Burns. Somehow my cousin Nigel is involved, although not as an investor, I should think, since he has no money at all. My brother stands to profit substantially from letting the grounds for the filming.''

"That is about what I have learned. It looks like an exercise in futility, but we can't connect it up with the dead woman.'' Westron was glum. "Progress is very slow.''

"Did you learn nothing from or about the dagger Geoff found?''

"Mr. Priam denies that it was his father's possession. Confirmed by a telephone call to Mr. Lawrence Priam. But we can't be absolutely sure. For the moment, we are assuming that it belongs to the maharajah or one of his party, and that points to an unfortunate conclusion. We'll have to see what he has to say.'' He looked at her expectantly.

"I was just going to run up for my chat with His Highness,'' Margaret said. "He will perhaps be at the polo field this afternoon for the so-called rehearsal. Your people might do well to approach him in his guise of polo consultant rather than the former ruler of an Indian state.''

"I intend to be there,'' Westron said, and sighed deeply. "It may turn out to be an ordinary domestic crime.''

"I do believe that the maharani was the intended victim, and not her husband,'' Margaret said. "She knew something. Mrs. Flood had a visit from her, and she hinted about some sort of discovery. Mr. Roach said she crept about the house listening at doors.''

"Likely the only thing she saw was her husband going off for a tête-à-tête with Jazmin Burns,'' Westron said.

"Ah, she told you about that.''

"No. Roach did. Miss Burns confided in him. Mrs. Domby, the housekeeper, saw them as well.''

"Mrs. Domby?''

"Heard them rather, after dinner. She was going up to her room. She also claims to have caught a glimpse of a lady in a sari, but she couldn't say whether it was one of the wives or a servant. Well, then. We'll be looking for you later, with the maharajah in tow. If it doesn't rain again, we'll be watching him gallop about.''

"I shall be among the gallopers," Margaret said.

"You play polo?"

"One learns the rudiments," she said. "Hold your mallet always in the right hand, and don't make a foul."

"True of most enterprises," Westron said. He strolled off toward the corner of the house.

Margaret was comforted to find her old riding boots, well polished, and the right sort of breeches for polo were in a closet in her room. A white jersey that could pass for a polo shirt was among other garments of different eras of her life stored in a drawer. She hoped Roach had thought to provide helmets and knee guards for his riders, and a mallet that was the right length for her.

Almost suitably dressed for the sport of kings, Margaret proceeded to the maharajah's suite. She was greeted at first knock by Doris, looking very grand indeed. She had donned a considerable portion of the traveling Tharpur jewels, and her sari today was a brilliant red, not the best color for a blonde of her sort.

"His Highness will receive you," Doris said.

"Woman, stop that beastly royal talk and go away. It has been very, very many years since I am seeing my little Margaret." The voice was familiar, elevated British English overlaid with a strong tinge of India.

"He is dressing for polo," Doris said. She shook her head. "Stupid sort of game, don't you think? Dangerous, too. I never cared for these horses and dogs. The people in the big house near our village used to go off fox-hunting. And they liked shooting the poor pheasants they raised from chicks so they could kill them off. I worked up there for a time when I was a girl, did I tell you? Thought it would be grand. It wasn't. I didn't care at all about being a servant. Now look where I am." Her smile was a trifle smug.

"Where was this place, I wonder?" Margaret said.

"Nowhere you've heard of," Doris said.

"Devi, go away jolly quickly, so I can speak privately with

Margaret." The maharajah was beginning to sound impatient.

"I am gone, beloved," Doris trilled. "I will be at the field to watch you ride."

Margaret looked about the room after Doris had departed. In its usual state, it was a tasteful masculine suite with a sitting room, bedroom, and dressing room, and a winding stair up to a tower room in which one could sit at ease and view the landscape in the direction of the village and beyond it to the farms. The room had now been adjusted to suit the more extravagant tastes of a maharajah. The new carpets that had been laid down were fine orientals, and the tables were packed with photographs in silver frames—the maharajah on the polo field with the Prince of Wales, the maharajah on a decorated elephant, one of a group with Jacqueline Kennedy Onassis, as a young man posing behind a dead tiger. There were piles of silk-covered cushions on the floor, the sofa, the chairs.

"Dear little Margaret." The one-time Maharajah of Tharpur flung open the door and made an Important Entrance with hands outstretched. He had gained weight, but the beige skin of his face was unwrinkled, and his hair was still dark and slicked back as she remembered it. His nails were as beautifully manicured as ever. He wore spotless white breeches and a fine white cotton polo shirt. His knee-high dark brown polo boots were polished to a glow and probably cost many hundreds of pounds.

"It's lovely to see you again, sir," Margaret said.

"Sir? What is this 'sir'? I am only an ordinary old man without a kingdom. Goodness me no, there are no more fourteen-gun salutes for old Ram. The winds of time have blown it all away, like the winds blow the dust from our desert roads. Now my wife of so many years has been taken from me. She was my eyes and my ears. We ruled our state together until that was taken from me." He could not quite manage a mournful tear, though he did look momentarily downcast, but whether for the loss of his wife or his princely state, she could not determine.

"I am so sorry about Her Highness's death," Margaret said.

The maharajah raised his hand to forestall further condolences. "She was a very fine woman, very fine indeed. She sacrificed herself in the first line of defense against my enemies. Rajput women are very, very brave. She died a heroine."

He rapped smartly on a table. A small, ancient man in a short jacket and billowing white trousers darted out from the dressing room. His white beard was very long, and his red striped turban was very large. The maharajah sat and allowed the servant to strap on padded knee guards.

"Do you believe you are in danger, as has been reported to the police by Doris?" Margaret asked.

"There are always dangers," he said. "Persons who envy wealth, persons who fear one's popularity. There are always jealousies and rages. One cannot always trust even those who claim to be the most devoted." He waved the servant away.

"If there is danger, why expose yourself to it? Why not take yourself to some place where you are far better protected than here at Priam's Priory?"

He looked resigned. "I am not so foolish as to think the police are not a little suspicious of me. My protestations of innocence mean nothing."

"If you spoke to them, you could explain about Her Highness's handprints," Margaret began. The maharajah began to pace, his back to Margaret. "You were told of them," she said, "and you did understand. . . ."

"Little Margaret," he said, "I recall that you like emeralds." He was not going to answer her. Instead, he opened a gilt box in a silver mounting, and took out a gold chain with big round green stones set between the links. "This is for you, to commemorate my return to this house, where I spent so many agreeable days with your father."

"Oh, I couldn't accept it, Highness," she said, knowing that she was turning down a fortune. "Mummie wouldn't allow it, nor would Nanny."

The maharajah laughed heartily, and tossed the necklace back into its box. "Didn't Elizabeth scold me when I spoiled you children? That is the true English aristocrat. Principles, decorum, the right behavior.''

"Sir, you haven't answered my questions. Why not leave for a safer place?''

The maharajah pondered the question. Then he said, "My ancestors never turned their backs on danger. I shall face it bravely, as did my wife.''

"Could not Her Highness have been murdered for other reasons? There are,'' she said delicately, "many kinds of dangerous jealousies in a large household.''

"You are thinking now of Devi.'' He shook his head. "She is not like the maharani, but they led separate lives, and I saw that neither of them suffered. Devi is a good enough girl.'' He did not sound convincing, and Margaret imagined that Doris's star was in a descent.

"Are you sure of Doris?'' she asked.

"Indeed I am,'' the maharajah said. "She has too much to lose by causing me problems. Without me, she has nothing. With me—well, there are resources even she cannot imagine.'' He seemed pleased by this.

"Sir, whatever you think, I urge you to allow the police to interview you.''

"I do not wish to speak to them. This is none of their affair.''

Margaret was exasperated. "Highness, murder is not a private matter in England. You know that perfectly well. If you do not speak to the man from Scotland Yard, you will be taken away and required to endure the questions of ten or twenty or a hundred policemen in a place not of your choosing. Whatever privileges you once enjoyed no longer apply. And,'' she added craftily, "if you do not speak, the police will believe that you must be guilty, and they will expend a considerable effort to prove it. Do you want to face a trial in the English courts? A lifetime in prison, even if you are innocent?''

"It is absurd to think that I would murder my wife of forty years.''

"But if Miss Burns was with you that evening, it would prove—''

"Hush!" The maharajah looked quickly toward the door. "That is a private matter."

"Too many private matters here," Margaret said. "I am sure Doris knows that you find Miss Burns attractive. It is entirely possible that Doris is well aware of the time you spent with Miss Burns, since others in the house know of it, as do the police. And," Margaret added slowly, "Doris herself might have had some hand in Her Highness's death."

The maharajah paced some more. Obviously it had occurred to him that one woman might have wished to eliminate the other. "She is an impulsive girl," he said finally. "I was attracted to her spirit, which had not been dampened by the brutalities of her early life. She has been good company for me. Still, my domestic life has not been peaceful of late. She was eager to spend time in England, but since we arrived here, she has been nervous."

"Did she not know she was coming for an extended stay at the Priory?"

"It is not necessary for me to state specifically how long I plan to remain in one place. That is not the concern of these women. Where I go, they go."

"I see. And now that Her Highness is dead, what are your plans?"

"Plans? I shall see that the traditional rites are performed, when the police allow it, and later I shall visit the continent until the heat in India is less. I shall return to Tharpur for the winter months as always."

"I meant your plans for Doris."

"Very likely our life will continue as before, unless she chooses to remain here in her native country. She did not take to India as I was hoping."

So much for Doris's desire for a relationship based on generally accepted legal principles.

"Miss Burns is expressing an interest in seeing Tharpur," the maharajah said. "That would be very fine indeed. Perhaps I will be inviting her to visit when I return for the winter. It is delightful to be showing my country to new eyes." For all his royal pretensions, his purported riches, and his man-of-the-world posing, Margaret felt a bit sorry for him: a man of a different time at sea in a modern world that had no place for him. He was a lonely aging man now, prey to calculating women who had little use for the remnants of his heritage.

"About seeing Mr. Westron," Margaret said. "Shall I tell him you will speak with him after the polo rehearsal?"

Highness's mouth was set in a tight line. His dear little Margaret was presuming to tell the Maharajah of Tharpur what to do.

"Come now," Margaret said, "it will do you no good to be stubborn. You will tell him that you were innocently chatting with Jazmin Burns after dinner when your wife was stabbed. He will ask you if you own a rather grand dagger with a white handle with jewels set in a flower pattern. An old piece; Mogul, I judge."

The maharajah blinked. "A dagger?" His eyes darted toward a drop-leaf desk which held a heavy black Mont Blanc fountain pen, a daybook open to the current week with notations for the coming days, and a pile of papers held down by an ugly paperweight fashioned out of a yellow chunk of stone like a piece of thick window glass mounted on a metal base.

"I do not have such a dagger," he said.

"Not any longer, in any case," Margaret said. "Who might have taken it?"

"I do not have such a dagger," he repeated. "And no one enters these rooms without my permission, not even Devi."

"Very well, sir," she said, certain that there had been a dagger among his possessions. "Such a dagger has been found on the drive below your windows." She went to the door. "Please heed what I've said. You're my very old friend, and one of my father's greatest chums, Ram-Sam."

He blinked at the nickname, and then smiled. "I shall find time to see this policeman," the former Maharajah of Tharpur said. "You are correct. I have no right to hinder the efforts of the police. I have admired the efficiency and honesty of the British since I was a small boy. Ah, let us be forgetting all this trouble and go out to the polo field." He snapped his fingers. The old servant appeared with a polo helmet and gloves.

"I left off practicing years ago," she said. "I need your coaching so as not to make a fool of myself."

"You were a good rider," he said. "I have had my man exercising three old ponies that survived your father. They do not forget their training, but they are slow now. Remember when your father had a string of wonderful ponies that even these Argentinians would envy?" He had put aside his cares for the moment. "I have had a couple of good mounts sent down which I borrowed from a friend. I wish this filming to be a success."

"To insure that the money you have invested is well spent."

The maharajah laughed. "Oh my goodness, Margaret pokes her nose into everything. She hears everything." Then he said, "I shall miss Laxmi, but this is how matters go in life. Let us not be talking more of this business. Come along to the sport of kings."

Chapter 13

*M*argaret *and* the Maharajah of Tharpur bumped their way in her rental car along a rutted, grassy track to the polo field at the far end of the Priory's parkland. The old turbaned servant sat in the backseat behind with an armload of polo mallets sticking out the window, and a pile of equipment on the seat beside him: fresh shirts, extra boots, spurs, and helmets. There was even a covered wicker picnic basket that exuded the faint scent of coriander.

The field, three hundred yards long and a hundred and fifty wide, was lined on one side by a few huge gnarled oaks that were all that remained of the ancient forests that had covered the land from the Stone Age. On the far side of the field, the deep woods that had grown up in more recent eras began.

The rain had finally stopped completely, and a pale sun struggled to show itself from behind thinning clouds.

The scene around the oaks was bustling with activity, a rather good imitation of a film company going about its business. Geoff could be seen with his camera, high atop a crane-like structure from which he would shoot the action on the field. A young woman had set up a table holding polo helmets, colored sashes, and a pile of mallets, while a youth and the older man she had seen at work in the drive were lugging pieces of equipment back and forth under the direction of Quintus Roach. He carried his riding crop and, of all things, a megaphone.

Nigel swung a mallet as he and David examined a group of ponies, one of them held by Potts. A groom was adjusting the saddles and bits, while Jazmin, now attired in skin-tight white riding breeches and a silk shirt with a plunging neck, lounged seductively in a canvas director's chair. At the far side of the field, four riders in green shirts were practicing their shots. No doubt these were the extra riders Roach had hired for the occasion.

Inspector Westron's sober black sedan was parked near the edge of the field beside the local constable's police car. The two men sat together in Westron's vehicle to watch the field. Margaret looked about for Phyllis and Lester Flood, but they had not yet arrived, nor had the crimson-garbed Doris or the reluctant Chloe.

Margaret headed for Nigel and David. The maharajah headed for Jazmin.

"Cousin Maggie, it seems like old times, you and me galloping across the grass in pursuit of a tiny rubber ball."

"I don't remember many such occasions, Nigel," Margaret said, "but your memory has always been acuter than mine."

"I'm not sure I can remember even the grosser points of the game," David said. "Off side forehand, near side backhand, neck stroke . . ." He walked away muttering to himself.

"Where do you suppose the devoted Chloe has got to?" Margaret asked. "She was reluctant to participate, but I thought surely she'd be here to observe the action."

"I caught sight of her in the library reading General Vickers's *Practical Polo*," Nigel said. "I don't think David shares the lady's intentions, do you? One notices the nuances in a couple's relationship. The right reading of people often comes in handy." He raised his mallet to the proper upright at rest position. "Too heavy for me, I think, although we don't actually have to hit the ball. Just come cantering down the field and avoid being killed. Practice for the heart-stopping action to be filmed in dynamite color for a boffo box office."

Margaret looked at him in amazement.

"Roach's words, actually," Nigel said. "These movie people speak a language of their own. Not to mention following rules of conduct that even I occasionally find reprehensible." He indicated Jazmin in head-to-head conversation with the maharajah. Margaret noticed that Ram-Sam had a possessive hand on the star's arm. "Look at that: one wife barely cold, and the other inflamed. Where is Doris, I wonder? She ought to be here to protect her turf."

"Nigel," Margaret said slowly, "about Doris and you. Actually about you and everyone. Your name pops up with truly alarming regularity."

"Mmm." He squinted up into the brightening sky. "It looks to turn quite fair."

Margaret was not to be deterred. "The maharajah and Doris, Roach and the Floods. Not to mention the gentlemen of the press, which is another story entirely."

"One gets about," Nigel said. "It's a hard world out there. You and David are lucky. The children of a peer with the family estate and the family treasures to back you up. I have had to do what I could to make my way. Seek out my own treasure, as it were. I'm good at reading people and picking up useful information. Information is valuable if properly used. Silence can be paid for, news can be profitably shared, and some very good investment possibilities can turn up. But—" he turned to her with an engaging grin "—I don't murder people."

Nigel strolled away to intrude on His Highness and Jazmin. Margaret watched him go. Information? Paying for silence? She didn't like the sound of that. It was too much like blackmail, but then, Nigel had never been hesitant about turning something of value into cash. A few Indian jewels sold, a few business ventures arranged, some secrets that would remain secret for a price. Very logical.

The maharajah left Jazmin to mount a fine-looking horse that was surely not one of the aging Priam polo ponies. His servant stood by patiently until the princely feet were in the stirrups, and the reins were in Highness's hands. Roach approached the prancing horse warily, and the maharajah leaned down to confer.

The maharajah then cantered away, showing the form for which he had been famous in his ten-goal polo heydey. Roach roared mightily through his megaphone: "Practice now, ladies and gentlemen. Lady Margaret, Lord Brayfield, Nigel Priam, pick up your gear pronto and get out on the field with His Highness. You other people stay back near the trees. This is only a rehearsal, but spectators will stand back. Thank you very much." He strutted toward the camera crane with riding crop under one arm and megaphone under the other, the very picture of the master of the cinematic universe.

The maharajah rode back to Margaret. "I have instructed Nigel Priam to take the first position. I would normally be number one, but I must observe. Margaret, you will find a helmet and a horse, and ride in the second position. David will ride in the third position, and I shall be the second back for the purposes of our exercise. Where is David?"

He leaned down and spoke in an unknown tongue to the old servant, who nodded and disappeared into the growing crowd of onlookers—village people and farm families, Ted and Lys from the Riming Man, strangers who might be connected with the village fair, and two or three men who looked suspiciously like members of the press. Nigel took a helmet from the wardrobe lady and mounted a pony held by Potts. He saluted Margaret with his left hand and cantered off toward the far end of the field, taking a few practice swings with his mallet. He seemed to be quite at ease.

Margaret tried on the helmet she was offered, adjusted the chin strap, and found that it was almost a good fit. She felt an innocent thrill of excitement as she mounted the pony. Polo had both glamour and danger, and she was keen to see if she remembered the fundamentals she had learned from her father. Reins in her left hand, her mallet held upright in her right, she cantered after Nigel. Her rather aged horse was surprisingly animated, perhaps by distant memories of rigid training and the excitement of the game. It would be all right, she decided. She turned her left shoulder so that she leaned out over her pony, stood in the stirrups, and swung the mallet at an imaginary ball.

"Excellent, excellent!" The maharajah galloped past her, headed for Nigel at the end of the field, two hundred yards away.

Margaret pulled on the reins to turn the pony to the right, and it responded as though it were still in its youth at the peak of training. She looked back toward the cherry picker, where Geoff was scanning the field through binoculars. One of the film crew was attaching cables to a generator and moving lights into position for later close-ups of the lovely Jazmin. The wardrobe lady had acquired a clipboard and was now the script girl, busily taking down Quintus Roach's flow of words. Westron and the constable had gotten out of the car and stood at the edge of the field. She caught sight of Jazmin's blond head in the middle of a crowd, possibly forcing her autographs on her English fans. Doris in her red sari had not yet arrived; at least she was not in the forefront of the spectators.

Margaret joined the maharajah and Nigel at the end of the field.

"We will not wait for David," the maharajah said. "He is probably bringing his young lady from the house. Such is young love that it makes one forget the clock. Now, we will ride down the field as though we are pursuing the ball toward the goal, we are making our strokes one at a time. This is to accustom your ponies to the game after so many years in retirement. Let me just speak with the gentlemen Mr. Roach has engaged as the opposition team, so they will understand what we are doing." He rode off to instruct the extras.

"I should think," Nigel said, "that the practice is more for us poor humans than the horses. I'm rather enjoying this. I don't ride as much as I did as a youth. Living in London with but a few weekends in the country doesn't keep one up to scratch."

"When the rehearsal is over, Nigel, we must talk. This murder has to be cleared up."

"I know nothing of murder, dearest, although I have my suspicions. Oh no, I'll not tell. Not you, not the police.

Although I must say that I am becoming extraordinarily popular. You and the policeman and good old Doris have all begged for moments of my time.''

"It's mostly about Doris that I wish to speak. Does she know something the maharani discovered? Nigel, you must tell me.''

"Don't worry about Doris. She's a sharp one.'' Nigel grinned. "Like me, Doris sets her sights high. It's nothing that concerns you or your precious Priory. Trust me. Come along, let's get on with this farce. We will create the illusion Roach wants. We shall demonstrate the fabled Priam ability to rise to almost any occasion. I've been told that there will be no close-ups. What a pity. I should like to see myself on the big screen.''

"Oh Nigel, you know this film will probably never be finished,'' Margaret said crossly. "I don't know why we bother.''

"We're humoring His Highness. And Mr. Roach. And we are aiding David, who really should be here. I hope he didn't decide that this was an occasion he couldn't rise to. Bad form.'' Nigel took his place as a forward, while Margaret moved her pony into place behind him.

"Take it gently,'' the maharajah called out. "Go!''

Nigel spurred his pony and galloped toward the opposite end of the field, swinging his mallet at an imaginary ball. Margaret rode behind him, and she could hear the maharajah's horse bringing up the rear. Once begun, it was exhilarating to gallop furiously down the field toward the goal. She crossed in front of Nigel successfully and swung her mallet.

"Good show!'' Nigel called out as he passed her and put distance between them.

Suddenly in midfield, Nigel pulled up, and his old pony stopped and turned without hesitation. Margaret's own pony also stopped and turned at the pressure from the bit and her knee, so that her back was to Nigel when a shot cut through the air.

She turned her horse quickly and saw that Nigel had fallen to the ground. His pony galloped away riderless.

"Assassin!'' she heard the maharajah shout behind her.

There was a second sharp rifle shot. She saw the crowd scatter to safety in the shelter of the old oaks, behind cars, under the camera crane. The maharajah had already reached the edge of the field, dismounted, and vanished into the crowd. Westron and the constable waved wildly, and she realized that they were signaling to her to race to safety.

Margaret galloped to the edge of the field, slipped down from her horse, and found herself surrounded by excited people.

"From the woods over there, it was," someone said.

"Didn't see him, did you?" another said.

"Is he dead? Is it the earl? What a story!" This from one of the newspapermen, who started running across fields toward the house even as he spoke.

"Isn't someone going to help Nigel?" Margaret said. "He's injured." She grabbed Westron's arm as he directed people away from the field. "My cousin . . ."

"The constable is summoning medical assistance," he said. "We can't allow anyone to be exposed to a person with a rifle. . . ."

"Nonsense," Margaret said. "I can't leave him alone."

Fifty yards away on the green grass, Nigel lay on his back motionless. His pony had returned and was standing over him. It looked to Margaret an enormous distance to travel on foot with a murderous rifleman hidden away in the trees. Nevertheless, she starting running toward Nigel, keeping as low to the ground as possible. She expected at every second to hear another shot, but she only heard the distant high/low wail of a siren. She was nearly out of breath when she reached Nigel and fell to her knees, hoping the pony might obscure her as a target.

Nigel had been shot in the neck, and blood had soaked his white shirt. He was deathly pale. She leaned over him.

"Help is coming," she said. "Hang on."

He moved his lips. "Sorry, Maggie," he whispered, then gasped.

"It will be all right," she said.

"No," he said. "Not all right."

"Who could have done this? Did he mean to shoot you?"

"Ask . . . ask Doris. The maharajah . . ." Nigel closed his eyes. His breathing was very weak.

Three men with a stretcher chose to brave the rifleman, and were racing across the field. The blood from Nigel's wound was on Margaret's hands, her shirt, and her breeches.

Westron was running toward them in a crouch.

"Rock . . ." Nigel gasped.

"What?" Margaret said desperately. "Which rock?"

"No . . ." Nigel was fading fast.

"Step aside, ma'am," a stretcher man said. "We'll handle it."

"You men get moving. No more danger. The police are already going through the woods," Westron said. "The lad on the cherry picker spotted movement in the woods after the first shot, couldn't say who. Did Priam say anything, Lady Margaret?"

"Nothing really," Margaret said slowly. She took the reins of Nigel's pony and walked toward the edge of the field. Doris was still nowhere to be seen, but David was pushing his way through the crowd to Margaret's side.

Ask Doris. Ask her what?

Dear Nigel, too clever by half to the very end.

Chapter 14

"*Nigel died* before reaching hospital."

Margaret felt many emotions as she announced the news that had been telephoned to her by Westron. Her jolly, disreputable cousin, friend of her childhood, was dead. He had worn a morning suit and top hat to her wedding, and had taken her off for a long, boisterous pub crawl through London when her divorce was final. When her infant daughter had succumbed to a chronic illness, he had sent her a roomful of roses. He likely lived just barely this side of the law, but he shouldn't be dead.

The group assembled beneath the medieval arches of David's priory room was subdued. Chloe clung to David—yes, he claimed he had gone in search of her before the rehearsal, but they had missed each other. Jazmin and Roach stayed together, and apart from the others. The maharajah, convinced that he had been the object of the attack, had barricaded himself in his room. He had sent a reluctant Doris to represent him. She looked normal for the first time, donning Western clothes. She, too, sat as far from the others as possible, and kept her mouth firmly shut.

Margaret had already telephoned the news to Nigel's father. Uncle Lawrence had sighed faintly off in his little house in Woking, crammed with mementos of a long career in India. He had sounded sad and brave, and alone. His only son was suddenly dead, and his only daughter lived far away in Australia with a rancher husband and a flock of children.

"My boy gone, just like that," he had said. "We joked that he'd come to a bad end, but not murder."

"Come to us at once," Margaret said. "Or I can come and fetch you."

"I don't want to trouble you," Uncle Lawrence said. "Perhaps you could come down to London on Monday to meet me. The train goes right from Woking to Waterloo Station. I should have a new tie; Nigel would like that. I will take a taxi to Harrods and we'll meet there."

"At the escalators on the Hans Road side. One o'clock. Highness will be pleased to see you," she had said.

Uncle Lawrence managed a weak chuckle. "That old devil Ram-Sam. Those were the days." He paused. "I am forgetting. Her Highness died as well. Nigel told me."

Margaret said, "Uncle Lawrence, do you recall meeting a Doris Smith, a friend of Nigel's?"

"Doris. Yes, yes. Sweet little thing."

"She's here, saying she is Ram-Sam's wife." Margaret imagined her uncle sorting that out. "Do you know anything about her?"

"Nigel brought her here once or twice. She liked my pretty things and my stories about India, so I suppose she took to Ram-Sam. She cannot be his wife, though. Margaret, I believe I shall lie down for a while. My boy gone . . ."

Now Margaret looked at the silent people in the priory room, awaiting Westron's arrival, and wondered which of them might have killed her cousin and brought grief to an old man. At least the film crew had been taken care of with a bottle of whiskey provided by Margaret to take back to their caravans, to make up for her canceled invitation to drinks.

"I hope we're not too late." Phyllis Flood sailed through the door of the sitting room. "We had to let ourselves in. Your Harbert wasn't anywhere about." She stopped short at the sight of the serious faces before her. Lester nearly tripped over his wife as he followed on her heels. "Les almost drove us into . . ." She stopped.

"What's going on?" Lester asked.

"Murder is what's going on," Quintus Roach said. "This is an absolute disaster for me. One more murder and I'm outta here. You too, Jazmin."

"The same murder or another one?" Lester asked.

"Another one," Jazmin said. "Nigel Priam got shot down while he was out riding around the polo field by somebody hiding in the trees."

"Didn't you hear about it in the village?" David said from the depths of his chair.

"Hell, those people wouldn't tell us anything if they dropped the bomb," Lester said. "Anyhow, part of the ceiling caved in as we were leaving for the polo field, so we never made it. So old Nigel is gone. Who could have done it?"

Everyone looked at him.

"Hey, folks. It wasn't me," Flood said. "He was a greedy pain in the rear, but I could afford him easy."

"Now that Mr. Flood has mentioned the cost of Nigel," Margaret said, "I wonder how many of you were being blackmailed by him."

This silence was even longer, as people began to squirm.

"Someone official will be looking into that, I'm sure," she said.

"Excuse me, Lady Margaret." Harbert was at the door. "Mr. Westron would like Lord Brayfield to join him and the constable to inspect the guns."

David got up. "Good Lord, everyone has guns in the country. Farmers have them to shoot vermin, the local lads do a bit of poaching. Why assume it was one of ours? We keep the Purdey shotguns and the good rifles locked up, but I can't keep track of everything. Why didn't they ask you, Harbert?"

"I wouldn't know, m'lord." Harbert headed for the door.

"Go along quietly, David," Margaret said. "If the odd rifle was left carelessly in the mud room or if there are others kept in the estate buildings, tell the truth. I found that it pays in the end." She hoped, as her brother departed, that he would follow her advice. She couldn't forget that David both held the keys to the gun cabinets and was not in evidence at the polo field when the shots were fired. But then, neither were the Floods nor Doris. Not even Chloe was there.

David said at the door, "You have guns at Rime Manor, don't you, Flood?"

Lester was momentarily flustered. "Sure I do. I've been hunting most of my life." David smiled grimly as he left.

"Shut up, Lester, before they try to pin something on us outsiders." Phyllis was not at all happy. "I never trusted Nigel Priam an inch. That kind has a lot of enemies."

"Chloe, you weren't at the polo field either," Margaret said.

Chloe was startled. "Why, no. I mean, you surely don't think . . . I barely knew the man. I was reading in the library and lost track of the time. Actually, Nigel saw me there. Then I started off to find the rehearsal, but all the cars were gone. I certainly wasn't going to *walk*. And why not ask questions of *her* rather than me." Chloe thrust her chin in the direction of Doris. "I saw her coming into the house not all that long before I heard the ambulance. She was going up the big staircase."

"Really!" Doris stood up. "I have nothing to say. I must go to His Highness," she said grandly. "If the police wish to speak with me, they know where to find me." She flounced to the door in her fashionably cut slacks and expensive cashmere jersey.

"Well!" Jazmin said. "The queen has spoken. Long live the queen."

Doris turned back. "Nigel never asked me for a shilling," she said. "Never."

Westron looked weary when he returned with David, who was considerably less nonchalant than when he had left.

"I will want to speak to all of you privately," Westron said, "to get a clearer picture of your whereabouts at the time of the shooting."

Lester Flood opened his mouth to protest, but was silenced by a look from Westron. The inspector continued, "I was watching from the sidelines with the constable, so I know what I saw, and who I saw. Several of you were not amongst the spectators."

"We had nothing to do with this," Phyllis said indignantly. "I'm not going to let them try to pin these murders on us outsiders."

"Mrs. Flood, I am an outsider here myself," Westron said mildly. "I shall not 'pin' anything on you solely because of your national origin. I am interested in knowing where you were in case you noticed something that will help resolve the matter. Does that satisfy you? I hope, however, that no one will feel compelled to depart the area without notice to the authorities. Mr. and Mrs. Flood will naturally remain in residence at their house, and the rest of you here."

Chloe said, "Here? With a murderer loose on the land? I planned to leave in the morning."

"What about my movie?" Roach demanded. "Time is money. I've lost a day already, I've lost one of my riders. Okay, we can get along without Priam. But we've got to rehearse tomorrow morning to shoot in the afternoon, and then move on to our next location."

"Quint, I don't think you get it," Jazmin said. "Poor old Nigel is dead, and the inspector thinks one of us did it."

"It was some hunter who's a lousy shot," Roach said. "Happens all the time. Go look for somebody who was out shooting bunnies and hit Nigel instead."

"Perhaps in your films, hunters make grievous errors," David said, "but I can assure you that there are few 'lousy shots' hereabouts, and in any case, this is not the hunting season." David did not look happy. Possibly it had occurred to him that the latest murder was definitely going to hurt his chances of reaching Wimbledon by the men's finals.

"Mr. Roach, I suggest that you rely on the extras you brought in," Margaret said. "I think that the maharajah may have lost his taste for polo, whatever investment he might have made in your film. I formally withdraw from further participation."

She was becoming increasingly apprehensive at the knowledge that someone with hands bloodied by murder was close at hand, if not in this very room.

How to connect the marahani's death and Nigel's? She knew for certain that she and the maharajah had not fired the rifle, yet she did not know on what errand he had sent his servant, who had probably spent his entire life doing exactly what his master commanded, from loading his hunting rifles in the Indian jungle to polishing his boots to God knew what else. She couldn't quite imagine the old man plunging a dagger into the maharani's heart, but if he had thought it was Doris . . .

"Lady Margaret." Westron's voice jolted her out of her reverie.

"Sorry," she said. "My mind was wandering. It's been a very long day for me, with little sleep."

"The cook is setting out tea in the drawing room," he said. "I should like a few words with you while the others partake."

"Tea, everyone," Margaret said, and suddenly they were all milling about near the door, still looking uneasy about the prospect of questioning by Westron once they had tucked into their tea. Suddenly Lester marched out, and the others followed. Margaret got a hint of how Flood's decisive actions might well enable him to pave over a large part of the middle of America with parking lots for eager shoppers.

Westron said to Margaret, "The only two people I am certain did not pull the trigger are you and the maharajah."

"I was just thinking that," she said, "but suppose Highness had an absolutely faithful retainer to do his bidding."

"The old feller with the beard and turban? He seems an unlikely killer of either the lady or your cousin. We still haven't spoken to His Highness. We have had no opportunity to inspect his rooms to see if he harbors weapons. I hope you will take care, Lady Margaret,'' Westron said gravely. "Although His Highness is claiming that he was once again the intended victim, I think that Nigel Priam was the person who was meant to die. You were seen at his side, hearing his last, possibly revealing words.''

"Therefore I might be in danger? It hadn't occurred to me, but what do you suggest I do? Lock myself in my room like the maharajah?''

Instead of answering, Westron asked, "Exactly what did Nigel say?''

Margaret hesitated. Then she said, "I told him that it would be all right, and he said no, it wouldn't. Then he said, 'Ask Doris.' Then, 'the maharajah.' That was all. No, he tried to say something about a rock, but the ambulance men took him away.''

"What did he mean?''

"I don't know," Margaret said. She hesitated. "You knew, of course, that both he and my brother knew Doris in London, before she met Highness. She claims she made her way from some dismal village to the bright lights of the city, and with Nigel's help—and my brother's—found herself uplifted to the fringes of international society.''

"It's odd, you know," Westron said.

"Odd?''

"We had roughly the same story from her, and we've tried to trace her back to this village she mentioned. No luck. She says she was an orphan, and has no relatives, but no one knows anything at all about her. I shall have to ask your brother about this.'' He was put out that David had not mentioned his previous acquaintance with Doris. His proper diplomatic demeanor was not holding up under the stress of two murders.

"I don't suggest you lock yourself behind thick doors, Lady Margaret, but please be careful. Don't wander about alone. And if there is anything to be asked of Doris, the police will do it—not you. I'm afraid I'll have to trouble you again tomorrow, when matters may be a bit clearer.''

"I will take care," she said. "I think I would rather not

join the others. I shall take tea with Mrs. Domby in the kitchen. You don't suspect her, do you?''

"No," Westron said. "Not yet."

Chapter 15

*W*hen *Margaret* entered the kitchen, she saw for the first time one of the Indian entourage. A small, dark woman in sari and bangles hunched over as she fled bearing a large covered dish. Margaret caught a whiff of Indian spices as she passed.

"Don't pay any attention to her," Mrs. Domby said moodily. "None of them speak a word of English." She was puttering aimlessly about the big kitchen. Old plans of the house showed the kitchen elsewhere, but in Edwardian times it had been relocated to its present position, overlooking the drive, the better to attract and keep excellent cooks.

Margaret's mother had seen it thoroughly modernized, so that by the time Mrs. Domby had risen through the ranks to her present lofty position, there was a six-burner cooker and a spacious refrigerator. Her complaints that she needed a big deep freeze had, however, gone unheeded. Instead David reminded her that London was not far away, and the village shops carried staples.

Margaret sat down at the huge table in the center of the room beneath a circular iron chandelier that quaintly still held candles rather than being wired for electric light. The table had been constructed of thick pine planks, scrubbed nearly white over the years by the hands of kitchen maids.

"A body could be killed in her bed," Mrs. Domby said. "It's these foreigners. You shouldn't be consorting with them, Lady Margaret." She poured Margaret tea from a blue and white teapot that was part of the collection of fine old Chinese export porcelain that filled the cupboards along one of the kitchen's walls. Mrs. Domby liked her little luxuries.

"Mr. Harbert!" Mrs. Domby raised her voice, then shook her head. "He was here a minute ago. He's probably serving our guests whiskey instead of a decent cuppa. Tilda!" Again, there was no answer. "And that one is probably hiding under her blankets. I can't run this place with no help. Harbert's gone queer, he has, what with the comings and goings and all the troubles. I remember how well Mr. Noakes coped with everything, never turned a hair when something went wrong. I was so impressed, even as a girl." She patted her hennaed hair with girlish coquetry. "I started as a maid when you were just a little thing, and Lord Brayfield had just been born."

"It has been a long time, hasn't it? You've been here all my life."

"And didn't I wish I could be your nanny instead of dusting and scrubbing and fetching? We had a nice little group here in those days. Then Mr. Noakes died suddenly, and your father brought in Mr. Harbert from some big house in the east, near Norwich. Not the duke, of course. Then your father died, and your mother just two years later."

"And my husband and I parted, and I went off to America. Not a happy tale."

"If I didn't know better, I'd say there's a curse on this house. The ghosts prove it. They're always about listening, like old Her Highness. They know when to show themselves, just when people's minds are troubled."

"I did see the gray lady today," Margaret admitted. "In the music room."

"There, you see." Mrs. Domby put her hands to her cheeks and shook her head. "And then Mr. Nigel died. A lovely boy, he was. I never believed the tales they told of him. He was as sweet as could be to me."

"And never had two pence to rub together," Margaret said, "and if he perchance did, he spent them."

"He was doing very well of late," Mrs. Domby said. "He told me himself that he'd found a very promising business enterprise. It was only a matter of time and all would be as right as could be. Such a tragedy, being struck down before he came into his own."

"Business, you say? Did he explain?"

"Something to do with His Highness," Mrs. Domby said. "Mr. Nigel has been popping in since the Indians arrived. He was being very free with financial advice, as though he was some kind of stockbroker from the City. I even saw him and Harbert sitting down together in the library." She sniffed considerable disapproval. "Said he was getting investment advice from Mr. Nigel. Fancy him talking about investments. That sort of familiarity would not have been allowed in Mr. Noakes's day. Strict, he was. Knew how to behave with his betters. Here now, have a bite of the nice jam tart. I know you don't get a decent tea in America. And Lord Brayfield told me that he can never get real marmalade in New York. You'd better stock up while you're here."

"I might stay on for a time," Margaret said. The tea was hot and strong, and the jam tart was just the way she remembered it.

"That would be lovely," Mrs. Domby said. "But don't you have a young man over there?" She eyed Margaret expectantly.

"I did," Margaret said, "but no longer. In any case, I want to be sure all this trouble is cleared up before I leave."

Mrs. Domby nodded understandingly, then cocked her head. Margaret, too, heard the sound of motorbikes roaring into the drive.

"Up the back stairs," Mrs. Domby said quickly. "Through your brother's room. It has to be the press boys from London. Mr. Harbert!" This time, Harbert did appear from the pantry. "Don't let one of those press people past the front door. Not one. We don't need any more nasty stories in the newspapers."

"I will see to it," Harbert said.

Margaret drew back the curtain of the small window that looked directly onto the drive and the front door. Two motorbikes and a car had pulled up almost to the steps. The constable addressed a group of men, ignoring their shouted questions. Quintus Roach hovered behind the constable, with an ingratiating smile. Perhaps he had decided that even bad publicity for his muddled epic was worth it. Margaret dropped the curtain, and carried her teacup up the stairs, through her brother's dressing room, and into the comfort of her own room.

The sun was just setting, June days being very long. She sat in a chair before the windows and thought.

If the rifle that had done the deed could not be found, where was it? The police, she understood, had thoroughly covered the woods where the shooter had stood with a wide view of the polo field, and had not found a gun. He—or she—must have been a good shot to hit a man on horseback.

The knife that had probably killed the maharani and stopped her tale from being told had been missing, and then it was easily found in an obvious place. Where would the rifle turn up?

Suddenly she was very tired. This endless day had begun the day before in New York, had brought her across the Atlantic, and had thrust her into a complicated situation crowned by murder.

She placed her teacup carefully on the table beside her chair and closed the curtains. Within minutes, she had taken to her bed, and was soundly asleep as night came.

"Lady Margaret . . ." Mrs. Domby's firm voice penetrated through Margaret's deep sleep. "There's a policeman to see you."

Margaret shook herself awake and squinted at the clock beside her bed. A bit past ten. Then she realized that it was morning.

Mrs. Domby bustled about, opening the curtains. "I came myself instead of sending Tilda," she said, "because of who it was."

"Couldn't he see David instead? What on earth do the police want with me now?"

"He asked for you specifically," Mrs. Domby said.

Margaret groaned.

"What shall I tell him?" Mrs. Domby waited at the door.

He couldn't be local, or Mrs. Domby would have mentioned it. It couldn't be Westron, or she would have named him. Perhaps Scotland Yard had determined that a more senior person yet was required.

"He's an American," Mrs. Domby said.

"American?" Margaret was wide-awake and out of her bed.

"Doesn't look like any American policeman I've ever seen on the telly. Wears those blue jeans and no tie, just a jacket."

Margaret was scarcely listening as she rummaged about for clothes, a comb, and makeup.

"I'll be down presently," Margaret said. "Have Harbert fetch coffee, or whatever he wants. I won't be a minute."

"I've had him wait in the Great Hall," Mrs. Domby said. "It's so impressive, don't you think?"

"Yes, yes it is. He's a friend from New York. I suppose he'll be staying. Could you see that his cases are taken to . . . ? Goodness, all the important bedrooms are occupied."

"I'll put him in the little blue bedroom. It's small, but I'm sure he will be comfortable," Mrs. Domby said.

"That will do," Margaret said. The blue bedroom was usually resorted to when there were simply too many guests at the Priory. It was just across the hall from Margaret's room.

De Vere was standing in the middle of the Tudor Great Hall, gazing up at the dark beams and the sets of antlers placed high on the walls. An earlier generation of Priams had been keen on lugging back trophies from shooting holidays in Scotland.

"Hullo, my dear," Margaret said, entirely flustered at the sight of him. "However did you manage to find me?"

De Vere grinned. "Our Prince Paul is your devoted friend," he said. "He managed to track me down in the pursuit of my official duties to tell me that you had left New

York, perhaps forever. He took the trouble to write out lengthy instructions, with details of flights to London and exactly how to reach Priam's Priory.''

"But he has no idea how to get here," Margaret said. Now that the shock of his appearance had worn off a bit, she thought it would be nice if he made a move to embrace her, having come all this way to find her. Perhaps the grand surroundings intimidated him.

"Those young women at the bank where Paul works still believe that he is a genuine Prince Charming, so they do his bidding instantly. In this case, researching his request for complete directions. I had some time coming. . . . Margaret, I've been a coward. It was easier to hide behind work than to face up to us . . . getting close." De Vere was not good at this sort of thing, but he was braver than she. "So I caught a late plane last night, and here I am for a short crime-free vacation. Its length depends on you.''

"Oh, goodness!" Margaret was touched by his words, but he was also the man who had vehemently voiced disapproval when she had become involved in murder in the past, and now the bodies were piling up at Priam's Priory at an alarming rate.

"What's wrong?"

"The first one happened before I even arrived," Margaret said quickly. "I knew *nothing* about it until I got here.''

"The first one?" De Vere said faintly.

Margaret took a deep breath. Two murders in the space of a few days might easily provoke a reaction more severe than mere disapproval.

"It was terrible," she said, and hoped for sympathy tinged with mercy. "The senior wife of the maharajah who is staying here was killed two days ago.''

"Killed, you say?" De Vere looked stern. "Dare I ask if it was an accident?"

"Well . . ." She decided that she could not avoid the truth. "Actually, no. And then there was the second murder.''

"I see.''

Since De Vere continued to show reluctance to embrace her in the midst of the Great Hall's splendors, she made the necessary move. As she wrapped her arms around him and felt him pull her closer, she whispered in his ear, "The maharani was stabbed, the other one was shot yesterday. My cousin Nigel." Then she added reluctantly, "A sort of blackmailer, I think."

"Oh, Margaret," De Vere murmured. "I cannot let you out of my sight."

"It really has nothing to do with me," Margaret said. "I was a bystander. Scotland Yard is on the job, and now that you're here . . ."

"Not a chance of any help from me," he said. "I gave up murders long ago, except for the occasional rubout resulting from business differences."

Suddenly the doors opened, and Harbert appeared bearing a tray with a silver coffeepot and cups. Margaret and De Vere stepped apart, but he continued to hold on to her hand.

"Thank you, Harbert," she said. "You may leave the coffee on the table."

"Very good, m'lady." Harbert eyed De Vere. No doubt Mrs. Domby had gleefully shared the information that Margaret's visitor was a policeman from America.

"Mr. De Vere has the blue room," Margaret said.

"It has been taken care of, m'lady." Harbert departed.

"I couldn't imagine you staying anywhere but here," Margaret said. "The only rooms hereabouts are at the Riming Man, and Ted must have filled them up with press people eager to write up the sordid murders at the Priory."

"I stopped at the pub for directions," De Vere said. "Quite a few people about." He helped himself to coffee. "I am about done in. I came straight here from the airport, largely driving on the wrong side of the road."

"Largely?"

"On the highways, it was fairly obvious where one was supposed to be even if it didn't feel right, but the back roads to your village and the house are remarkably narrow. There is no right or wrong side of the road, only a road."

"I'm so glad you're here, Sam. I've got a terrific lot of things to tell you, but they can wait for now. You'll like the man from Scotland Yard. He's a sort of soothing man sent down to keep the first murder from becoming an international incident involving persons friendly with our Royals. I think he now may be in over his head.''

"I was hoping simply to enjoy myself for a few days and then persuade you to turn your back on England and come home to New York with me.''

"I couldn't leave now," Margaret said. "Nigel was a member of the family, and my brother is something of a suspect. Not an obvious one," she added hastily. "There will have to be a funeral, and I'm supposed to fetch his father, my Uncle Lawrence, who lives in Surrey, near London. He's an old man and quite alone now.''

"I understand all that," De Vere said, "but think about it, will you?''

"Yes," Margaret said. "I will. Mmmm, there are a number of other complications here, by the way. We have people here filming some bits of a movie with Jazmin Burns, who is in residence.''

De Vere gave a low whistle. "She's here? There's someone I wouldn't mind having a close look at. I'd say she's a dangerous woman in her own right, if the papers tell the truth, but I don't picture her as a murderer.''

"I doubt it. She seems pleasant enough. How bad could one be with a guru named Chuck? Let's not talk about murder anymore for a time.''

Chapter 16

The doors to the Great Hall were flung open and Chloe Waters marched in.

"I heard voices," she said. "Is David here? I simply *must* leave. I could run over to stay at Figge Hall with Mummie and Daddy. It's not that far, and Daddy wants me clear of this mess, but no one seems willing to give me leave to depart." She sounded just a teensy bit put out that anyone would dare to forbid her to do whatever she chose.

"I haven't seen David today," Margaret said. "Chloe, this is my friend Sam De Vere from New York."

"Ah." Chloe sized him up with a critical eye. Not the aristocracy of America, her look seemed to say, but good-looking in an offbeat way. Not one of her kind, but appealing. "Mr. De Vere, is it? I know some De Veres in Essex. . . ."

"Not my family, I'm afraid," he said with rather more good humor than Margaret would have expected.

"I see," Chloe said. "I'll just run along and find David. He has to do something." She clearly meant her particular situation.

"If we have to stay about for a time while the police clear up the murders," Margaret said, "no harm done. We'll all go to the village fair. The police can't object to that. And I'll be driving to London the day after tomorrow to fetch Nigel's father. Perhaps the police will see their way to letting you go with me—unless you'd care to stay on for Nigel's funeral.''

''Heavens no!'' Then Chloe realized that her tone was not entirely right for speaking of the death of a relative of her marital prey. ''I mean to say, I couldn't intrude.''

''We'd be so glad to have you with us,'' Margaret said, ''and I'm sure it would mean a great deal to David.''

''I doubt it,'' Chloe said crossly. ''He didn't care a bit for Nigel, and I know for a fact that Nigel was causing him no end of trouble about the filming fees and arranging things with the Floods.''

''I suggest you not broadcast that news too widely,'' Margaret said. ''The police might get the idea that David wanted to see Nigel out of the way.''

''What an idea,'' Chloe said. She turned to De Vere. ''We're all hoping these murders are cleared up quickly. The police are such idiots, don't you think?''

''Not all policemen, surely,'' Margaret said wickedly.

''All of them,'' Chloe said firmly.

''Did I mention that Mr. De Vere is with the New York City police?'' Margaret said.

Chloe made a rapid recovery. ''Naturally things are different over there,'' she said. ''A much better class of people in the police.''

''We like to think so,'' De Vere said cheerfully. Chloe withdrew hastily before she stumbled again.

''She's someone my brother likely will not marry,'' Margaret said. ''But of course, the police have no reason to think she's the murderer. She's far more concerned about losing her grasp on the title of countess.''

''I suppose you've pegged the murderer, well ahead of the police,'' De Vere said. He was half-teasing, half-curious.

''As a matter of fact, I have a suspicion,'' Margaret said slowly, ''but not one bit of proof. Nigel might have told me, if I'd asked him the right questions before it was too late.'' When De Vere looked at her questioningly, she explained about Nigel's last words in the middle of the polo field.

''Don't you think you might be in danger,'' De Vere said,

"if you were seen by this murderer hearing the victim's last words?"

"The possibility has been mentioned," she said. "I say, do you carry a gun?"

"Certainly not! I came on a vacation. But I did bring my wits."

"That's something," Margaret said. "I ought to have a bodyguard, don't you think? You could stick to me like Scotch-tape."

"I think I get your drift," De Vere said. "But I will have nothing to do with solving any murders. And neither will you," he added firmly. "Tell that to your Scotland Yard pals."

"But you will come along and meet Westron. Professional courtesy. Then I'll leave the police to their labors and show you about the estate."

"Well! Someone new to join our game of Catch the Killer."

Jazmin Burns posed at the doorway, hand on hip. Margaret thought she had seen that sort of entrance in an old Bette Davis movie on television.

"This is Detective De Vere from New York," Margaret said. "He's been dying to meet you."

"Then I'm happy to meet him," Jazmin purred. "But be careful, hon, dying is getting to be an epidemic around here. I'm off to find some breakfast. I couldn't persuade the help to bring any to my room this morning. Too busy, your butler said when I caught him upstairs doing nothing to speak of, but I guess my magnetic charm wasn't working. I ask you, is that a way to run a grand house like this?"

"No," Margaret said, "but these are uncommon times."

Westron, at his post in the library, was momentarily taken aback at being introduced to a member of the New York police.

"Mr. De Vere's arrival was entirely fortuitous," Margaret said hastily. "He had no idea that he would be arriving in the midst of a murder."

"Two murders," Westron said gravely. "You Americans are said to have quite a lot of experience with multiple homicides."

"My colleagues do," De Vere said. "I haven't dealt with murder for some time, not since Margaret and I met a couple of years ago. She kind of dampened my interest in that particular crime, although in my younger days on the force, I had to collect the remains of youthful mayhem and clear up body parts resulting from domestic violence. I have no intention of becoming involved in these murders you have on your hands. I'll leave you two to your business. The less I know of it, the better." Westron seemed relieved.

"You could walk about yourself for a time," Margaret said, although she longed to be the one to show him the Priory's grounds. "There's a little classical temple down by the lake. Neither it nor the grounds there have been kept up, but it's charming. I'll meet you there. Harbert will point you in the right direction."

Harbert hovered outside the library doors to receive Margaret's instructions.

"This way, sir," he said to De Vere. He proceeded solemnly toward the front entrance. De Vere looked back at Margaret, and she thought he winked at her. High on his list of dislikes relating to the aristocratic way of life were imperious butlers.

"I'll find you in a bit," she said. In spite of the troubles swirling around Priam's Priory, she was beginning to feel quite cheerful. The Atlantic was not so formidable after all.

"Mmm," Westron said. "Interesting that your friend mentioned domestic violence. I'm thinking along those lines." He appeared to be reviewing the maharajah's somewhat irregular arrangements. "I, too, have not recently been on many murder cases. In fact, some other men from the Yard, CID people who know their way around murder, are on their way to take over. I'm keeping our end up until they get here. We don't want to see the maharajah take it into his head to cut his way out with flashing swords."

"I just don't see His Highness doing murder," Margaret said, "even via his servant."

"The dagger was beneath his windows," Westron said. "Or his second so-called wife's windows. Now, however, neither of them will speak to us. She won't open her door. Wouldn't even answer the butler when I had him go up and ask her to come here for a chat. Well, now that you're here, Lady Margaret, perhaps we can go over again the events of yesterday afternoon."

Westron methodically reviewed her actions from the time she arrived on the polo field to Nigel's last words.

"I'm sure Doris holds the key," Margaret said.

"A pity that your cousin who knew her so well is dead."

"And is she safe? If Nigel knew something about her—"

"We are keeping watch. My colleagues will see that she tells us that something."

"I'm hoping to drive down to London to bring Uncle Lawrence here for my cousin's funeral. Nigel is to be buried in the family plot."

"There's no problem with you going," Westron said. "You are not a suspect." He turned his back on her and gazed up at the books he continued to find engrossing. "I'd like to suggest that your policeman friend accompany you. In fact, I'd feel easier if you kept fairly close to him. I understand that he doesn't want to become involved in our investigations, but one assumes that after working in the midst of New York carnage, he has experience in protecting his— and your—back."

"That is true," Margaret said, "and there's nothing I'd like better than to have him always at my side."

"That's settled. As you sent him off to view the sights of the estate, I'd also suggest that you enlist Mr. Harbert to accompany you to where he might be found."

"No," Margaret said. "Not Harbert, I think. It would be . . . beneath his dignity. Potts will accompany me."

She and Potts found no sign of De Vere waiting for her beside the chipped marble columns of the round building that had once sheltered Priams philandering with buxom wenches on sunny eighteenth-century afternoons.

"I'll be in safe hands now, Potts," Margaret said. "Mr.

De Vere will see to me. He must be walking about along the stream."

"Very good, m'lady. It's a pity I don't have the men to keep up this part of the estate. It's gone all wild since the war." Potts meant the Second World War, both during and after which both landscape helpers and money were in short supply. Margaret had only seen old drawings of how the spot had looked when it was in its prime: ladies in billowing gowns and lace caps strolling on manicured grass with gentlemen in frock coats, while decorative swans paddled in the lake.

"Doesn't stop people from coming around, though," Potts said. "I saw this Mrs. Flood from Rime Manor crashing through the underbrush and clapping her hands like a soul bereft of her senses at the sight of the old building. I'm thinking picturesque sights are damaging to these Americans. Then one of the Indian ladies tried to build a fire here to cook when Mrs. Domby chased her out of the kitchen." Potts shrugged. "I sent her about her business that time. Don't like fires around the estate. There's no telling what these Indians are going to do. Not that they're much trouble around the house. Scarcely see a sight of 'em. But they like to burn that incense business. Mr. Harbert took me up to their floor to fix a bit of wiring that went wrong in His Highness's room. I could hardly breathe for the smell."

Margaret interrupted him. "Thank you so much, Potts."

He trudged off whistling.

Margaret stood in the middle of the circular building, open on all sides except for the widely spaced columns supporting the dome. She gazed out upon the encroaching trees and beyond to glimpses of meadows and faraway hills.

As the minutes passed, she began to wonder what had become of De Vere. She stood up and scanned the wooded area surrounding the rotunda. She could see along the edge of the lake a faint reminder of a bricked walk now mostly covered with brambles and other wild growth.

She walked to the edge of the little building that opened directly onto the lake and dropped some six feet to the water. The lake had been artificially contrived when the rotunda was built by damming the stream, so it wasn't deep, but weeds had grown up on the bottom, and the water looked murky and forbidding. She raised her hand to shade her eyes. She thought she had caught a glimpse of De Vere in the trees on the other side of the lake.

She started to call to him when she heard the rifle shot and felt the sharp shower of marble where the bullet had struck the column above her head.

Lady Margaret Priam did not hesitate. She jumped, and hit the water with a resounding, somewhat painful splash, arms and legs outspread so that she wouldn't plummet to the bottom and its unknown dangers. She surfaced quickly and paddled close to the waterside wall of the rotunda as it descended into the lake. She dared not swim to the shore, where she might again become a target—if indeed a target she was. But if she waited too long in the water, whoever had thought to dispose of her would have a chance to creep up to the building and shoot again from above. She recalled a phrase she'd heard: "like shooting fish in a barrel." She didn't like the idea of becoming one of the fish.

She could only hope that someone at the house or about the estate had heard the shot and would come to investigate. She stayed very close to the greenish, slimy stones of the wall.

"Margaret!"

Margaret swallowed a distasteful mouthful of water in jerking her head up to look at the person standing above her.

"Sam, thank goodness."

"What are you doing in the water?"

"Come around to the edge of the lake and help me out," she said. She wasn't sure it was a good time to tell De Vere that she had been shot at. "Where have you been?" she asked as he gave her a hand to haul her out of the water.

"I started out to find this place, but somehow I got the directions wrong," he said. "I tramped through the underbrush and across meadows until I came upon the stream, and then followed it along to the lake and saw this thing." He brushed her wet hair back from her face and looked at her closely. "I heard what sounded like a rifle shot."

"You did," she admitted, and suddenly felt rather weak.

"It was likely someone shooting at a rat or a marauding rabbit, but I didn't stop to think before I jumped."

"I see," De Vere said. He took her arm protectively and scanned the trees and horizon. "No one visible now, but snipers are unpredictable."

"Sam, this isn't New York City," she said.

"Right. New York seems less dangerous."

She was feeling calmer. "I simply overreacted because of the murders. I do need to change my clothes rather urgently," Margaret said. "Then I'll show you about the estate. I'll stick close to you, my beloved bodyguard, I promise."

As they entered the house through a side door into the mud room, she could hear Quintus Roach far away shouting into the hall telephone to someone he had awakened in Los Angeles in the hours before the West Coast dawn. Apparently he believed that the louder the voice, the more readily it traveled across the ocean. Margaret paused to look at the gun cabinets. Everything seemed to be in place.

She had a strong suspicion, however, that the shot out of the blue had been specifically intended for her.

"These clothes are very disgusting," Margaret said. "Hang about somewhere, and I'll hurry. Ah, here's a companion for you. Wally, meet Sam De Vere. Show him around."

De Vere looked at the large black dog who gazed up at him, not quite ready to be friendly.

"It's all right, old boy. A friend of the family's."

She ascended to her room. How could she determine where everyone had been in the past hour or forty-five minutes? She quickly bathed away the stagnant lake water and put on a fresh blouse and slacks. One of her shoes was at the bottom of the lake; she decided to save the other to remind her of the day's event.

When she came downstairs, she peeked into the library. Westron was just dismissing David, who looked extremely put out.

She met her brother in the hall. "What sort of problem has arisen now, David?"

"It seems that I, along with Ram-Sam and Doris, continue to arouse the suspicions of the police."

Margaret would never have believed that she would ask the next question of her brother, but she had to be sure. "Can you tell me where you were in the past hour or so? I ought to say, can anyone vouch for your whereabouts?"

David looked at her as though she were crazed. "I have no idea if anyone would want to," he said. "I say, you're serious!"

"Someone shot at me at the thingy by the lake. I must know that it couldn't have been you."

David looked at her blankly, then laughed. "I had a long talk with Chloe; I was forced to go over some household accounts with Mrs. Domby. I spent considerable time with Westron. No, dear sister, I wasn't out shooting at you. What a bizarre thought."

"I needed to hear you say it," Margaret said. "Look, here's Sam De Vere, who's come to stay for a time."

"Ah, yes, De Vere," David said, no longer merely Margaret's brother, but the Earl of Brayfield greeting a distinguished guest. "Met you in New York, didn't I? Jolly good, enjoy yourself. Margaret, neither His Highness nor Doris will speak to the police. Westron's very ticked off. Go up and plead with them, will you? Take De Vere in case they decide to attack you. You've heard of our troubles, De Vere? Such a bore. Roach is going ahead with filming, Margaret. Must get to the polo field." David took himself off.

"Estate tour leaves as soon as I try to have a word with Doris," Margaret said. "Do you ride?"

"Horses? I have ridden," De Vere said cautiously. "I am not a mounted policeman, remember."

"We'll walk then, if you're up to it. Wally will probably manage part of the tour before he realizes that he doesn't have to exert himself as he did in the old days. And if Doris is worried enough about her own skin, she'll be a bit more forthcoming about things she hasn't seen fit to mention. I'll only be a moment."

The hallway upstairs was quiet. She paused to listen outside the door to His Highness's rooms, and was startled when Harbert emerged. He seemed unnerved to find her there.

"His Highness requested more Priory writing paper," he said. "He seems to be performing some religious ceremony in his dressing room, so I did not disturb him." Harbert seemed put out.

"No doubt related to his wife's demise," Margaret said. Harbert started toward the stairs but stopped when Margaret added, "Did you happen to notice anyone following me down to the rotunda after Mr. De Vere? I thought I caught sight of someone amongst the trees, but when I looked again, whoever it was had gone. Perhaps I'm beginning to see ghosts everywhere I look."

"I did not notice anyone leaving the house," he said. "The boys from the village have been playing games near the lake. I've advised his lordship to put a stop to it as the little building is not safe."

"How true," Margaret said. "It must have been the boys I saw."

When Harbert had safely departed, she knocked on the door next to the maharajah's.

"Doris? It's Margaret. I need to talk to you."

There was no answer for a time, then Doris spoke on the other side of the closed door. "I don't have anything to say. Go away." She sounded strange.

"You can't hide forever," Margaret said. "We have to clear things up."

"There's a murderer running loose, and I'm not going to put myself in danger," Doris said. "I've bolted the door, and no one can get in. A girl has to look out for herself. Please go away."

Margaret shrugged. No answers here with a solid, bolted door between the two of them. Let the police break it down to reach her.

It was a relief to leave Doris—who would surely be safe for the moment locked in her room—and walk back out into the sunshine. It was a perfect English June day, with humming bees busy among the roses, and faithful Wally posing majestically on the steps. At his side was De Vere, looking off across the fields toward the village, where the square bell tower of the old church was just visible among the trees.

"Doris sounds frightened," Margaret said. "As well she might be." She sighed. "I did rather fancy shaking the truth out of her, but now I'll leave that to Westron. A few more questions from the police, and she'll tell all."

"Don't be so sure," De Vere said. "Not if telling means losing what she's achieved."

"There you are," Margaret said. "Too much to lose."

Chapter 17

It was near midnight when Margaret suddenly awoke in her big canopied bed. Something had startled her from an uneasy sleep. She sat up and listened, but could detect no sound anywhere in the house.

No one should be about at this hour. After his long flight from the States and a tramp over the estate, De Vere had retired early to catch up on his sleep. Mrs. Domby had provided them with a sustaining tea of sandwiches and cakes in the seldom-used drawing room, so they hadn't had to encounter any of the other residents of the Priory. Margaret herself had gone to her bed soon after with a fairly boring Iris Murdoch novel she hoped would put her to sleep and keep her from thinking about a murderer in the house.

In the darkness now, Margaret got out of bed and went to the windows to pull back the curtains. Rain clouds had again moved across the sky, so there was no starlight, no moonlight. She started back to bed, and froze. She walked carefully through to the door and listened. There was definitely a sound of movement on the other side of the door.

I do hate being terrorized in my home, she thought, then she opened the door. Wally stood outside, wagging his tail and almost grinning at the sight of her.

"You haven't forgotten, have you, old chap?" She let him into her room. "Here I was imagining a murderer or a ghost

141

at my door, and it was only my friend." Although the late Countess of Brayfield had specifically forbidden it, Wally had frequently managed to creep up the stairs to spend the night at the foot of Margaret's bed. Now he plumped himself down in his accustomed spot.

Margaret peered out around the hallway. No lights showed at the bottom of any of the doors, and silence reigned. It occurred to Margaret that she had only seen one member of the maharajah's entourage other than Doris and the old servant. True, she had heard voices, but the women never showed themselves about the house. But that wasn't right. They did come out of their rooms. Mrs. Domby allowed one of them in her kitchen; Potts had seen one at the rotunda. And someone with an Indian voice had answered her call from America before Harbert had taken over the telephone.

Something clicked faintly in the back of her mind. She was wide-awake now, and the pieces of the Priory murders began to come to her in a jumble.

She started with the old maharani listening at doors. This was a fact, stated by Roach, confirmed in a way by Mrs. Domby and Harbert. A tentative conclusion was that the night of her murder or earlier, the maharani had heard or seen something. She was, after all, the maharajah's "eyes and ears." Someone at Priam's Priory had discovered that she knew something and had silenced her. She had left a warning to His Highness with her handprints.

What had she seen or heard? Could it be about Jazmin? Margaret thought not. Nigel's last words and what she already knew of Doris made it more likely that it was about her. Nigel and Doris. Ambitious, possibly greedy, both of them having had to struggle to get where they were, and they didn't want to lose it. Domestic violence. Not wanting to lose something of value. A new suspicion nudged its way into her consciousness. She tried it out from several angles, and it seemed logical. She would have to be careful.

"How would you like a little adventure?" she said to Wally, who thumped his tail on the floor. Wally was agreeable to almost anything, except possibly a band of new puppies about the house. Fortunately, David was not a fanatical dog person, so Wally remained the aged king of all he surveyed.

She changed into jeans and a dark shirt, and pocketed a small disposable flashlight, which she had learned to pack whenever she traveled. "To the estate office," she said, and did not find it odd that she was conversing with a dog. "Duty calls."

She made her way down the back stairs in the dark. On the ground floor, a faint night light burned at one end of the corridor that ran parallel to the Great Hall, but she knew her way about so well that she could have found any room in the house with her eyes shut.

The estate office was on the ground floor, next to the mud room. The desk where David worked was littered with papers, but the file cabinets were orderly. She rummaged through folders of paid bills and reports on agricultural studies, Inland Revenue documents, heifer pedigrees, bloodlines of long-deceased polo ponies, correspondence with various estate personnel. It took her a while to find the files she was seeking, and when she had found them, they told her nothing.

What she was looking for was not there.

"To the library," she said, and Wally tagged along patiently. She was too wide-awake to return to bed just now, but she couldn't think of other leads to pursue. She made her way in the dark through the house, and only switched on lights when she entered the library.

Somewhere on the shelves lined with sturdy leather volumes was the folio-sized book in which generations of Priams and visitors had written about their encounters with the Priory ghosts. She found it among the volumes shelved near the floor. As soon as she saw the dark blue binding, she recognized it.

She settled down in a leather armchair to find the long account of the tragic woman who had become the Priory's ghostly gray lady.

"Mistress Clare was said to have died at the hand of her husband, Thomas Clare, who came to this house where his wife had been given charge of the children of the widowed

Earl of Brayfield. This was in the year 1801. Mistress Clare was met at the door by her husband, who accused her of dallying with the earl.''

The ink of the handwritten entry was a pale violet; the hand was a formal copperplate from the middle years of Victoria's reign, not many decades after the death of Mistress Clare. The account had been written out by a young man engaged by the then-earl to catalog his books, who had taken an interest in the ghostly appearances at the Priory.

''Mistress Clare was stabbed by her husband, who refused to hear her protests of innocence. As they had long been estranged, and Mistress Clare had been seen frequently in the company of the earl, at times when the children were not present, Thomas Clare escaped prosecution for the crime. It was deemed a reasonable response to the infidelity of his wife, although it was said that Thomas Clare was himself an unfaithful and vicious husband, and his wife had fled from him to find peace.

''The first known sighting of the ghost presumed to be Mistress Clare was on July 17, 1815. The personal maid of the countess met a fierce staring woman in the passage outside the ballroom, who soon vanished and sent the maid shrieking to her mistress.''

Following the brief history were entries in different hands over nearly two centuries: the sightings by the earls and countesses, governesses, and even a visiting clergyman, the dictated statements of downstairs maids and footmen, the enthusiastic accounts of ghost seekers lucky enough to have found what they sought.

''This spirit is frightening,'' went one entry from the 1890s. ''I dropped the basin I carried at the sight of it and lay abed for several days. I was shaken by the experience.''

The benevolent nun, seen more rarely, had correspondingly fewer pages. In the librarian's hand was written: ''Said to be a female member of the Gilbertine order. She haunts the ruins of the old priory and the places where buildings now vanished once stood.''

''The ancient religious lady, who is said to haunt our old stones, appeared to me last night,'' wrote the twelfth Earl of

Brayfield. "Our times have been troubled, at home and throughout the land, and I was in despair. I walk'd the long ruin'd corridor that was once a cloister'd hall and beheld in the moonlight a woman in the shadows with a pale and saintly face. She raised her hand in what I understood to be a blessing upon me, although we are not of the Roman faith. When I looked again, she was gone. I knew it must be the creature mentioned in the tales handed down by our family."

As Margaret glanced back into history, with Wally sleeping at her feet, far away from the library the dusty air stirred among the old stones of the Priory. A door opened and closed without a sound, and slowly, carefully, an indistinct figure moved through the darkness.

Margaret looked up suddenly from the book of ghostly sightings. It seemed to her that she had heard a faint sigh. Then she thought she must have imagined it. Wally had not moved. She was uneasy, however. She had felt so at home that she had forgotten there was likely a murderer in their midst, and she had promised to venture out only if De Vere was with her.

She listened again, and now she did not imagine it: a sound like a drawn-out breath as though the old house itself were sighing. All at once she felt an icy chill pass over her like a faint breath of cold wind. Wally whimpered in his sleep.

Margaret waited without moving, but nothing more occurred, if anything had occurred at all. Margaret turned back to the pages about the gray lady, and quickly wrote:

"Seen this day by Lady Margaret Priam: the ghost of the gray lady in the music room. I stepped into a circle of cold as I approached the figure, which was sitting in one of the chairs in the half-darkness. After a moment, it vanished, and warmth returned. It was seen also by Miss Jazmin Burns of Beverly Hills, California, U.S.A., who stated that she, too, felt the coldness."

Then she signed her name and dated her entry. The business of history at Priam's Priory had been taken care of. She glanced at the summary of the gray lady's tale. Domestic violence again. Very apt for the present situation.

Suddenly she felt she must see the place where the maharani had died. The need was so strong that she didn't care about being cautious.

"Come along, Wally. Let's take a look."

She made her way through the house to the silent, spotless kitchen, and let herself out the door that led to the garden on the one hand and the Nun's Walk on the other. The police seal on the door to the cloistered passage seemed to have been broken.

It's my house, after all, she told herself in justification for pressing on the old-fashioned latch and letting herself into the hallway.

The long space before her was totally black. It was damp and chilly, and there was a musty smell seeping up from the old earth beneath the flagstones on which she walked. She took out her pocket flashlight and shined it before her. The thin beam of light showed some yellow plastic strips at the end of the passageway, which marked the spot where the maharani had died, leaving her telling handprints. Margaret's eyes began to adjust to the darkness, so she could make out the shape of the hall and the arched window niches. She switched off her light.

Wally started to plod forward ahead of her, then stopped. He growled faintly deep in his throat, and Margaret grabbed his collar. On the flagstones a few yards ahead lay a long, slim object. She started to walk toward it, then quickly halted at the noise of scuffling footsteps on stone. Wally pricked up his ears, the mighty hunter alert at the sound and scent of his quarry.

Far down the hall she saw a shadowy figure in a long, dark robe. She caught her breath. The ghost of their nun was guarding the spot where the maharani had died. Margaret felt a shiver of fear, and did not move. Kindly or not, a ghost is a ghost.

The ghost raised its hands and then began to advance toward Margaret. It was menacing rather than kindly. She touched Wally's back, but instead of the raised hackles that had been his response to the gray lady's ghost in the music room, Wally was wagging his tail cordially. He had recognized a friend. It was not a ghost at all.

The figure was still moving toward her deliberately. Then it stopped suddenly. The area around it appeared to brighten for an instant. Margaret thought quickly. "De Vere," she called over her shoulder, "come quickly, and bring your gun." Wally started forward, but she held his collar.

But even as she was calling out, the figure was running away toward the far end of the passage. In the faint beam of her torch, she saw the dark shape retreating rapidly. It vanished in the gloom. She swung the beam around to every corner of the Nun's Walk, but there was nothing to be seen.

Then Wally growled and stiffened.

"Fine protector you are, when it's too late," she said. "Let's have a look at what was left behind."

Since Wally refused to follow, she walked alone toward the object on the ground. It was a rifle, with a worn stock but well enough cared for. Not a gentleman's hunting weapon, but easily a serviceable piece for a farmer or a gamekeeper. She did not doubt that it was the rifle that had killed her cousin and had been used to shoot at her, and like the jeweled dagger, it had been left in a spot where it might implicate someone. The only exit at the other end of the passage was through the door that led to David's private priory room. She wondered where her brother was at this moment.

She left the rifle where she had found it and proceeded toward the door that would take her directly to the columned room. She found that the door was firmly locked. The huge old-fashioned iron key was always left in the keyhole on the other side.

Margaret started to retrace her steps along the Nun's Walk to the door into the kitchen. Wally went ahead of her, eager to be gone. She stopped and looked back down the passageway. The clouds must have moved on, because a bit of moonlight through the window openings brightened the hall somewhat.

"Ohhh." A faint sigh escaped her. The creature was back, perhaps this time with a weapon. She could easily see the outline of a person at the far end. No, she could make out two pale figures against the dark walls of the Nun's Walk. One of them raised its hands in a wide, expansive gesture.

Suddenly a cloud covered the moon again, and both figures disappeared.

A trick of the moonlight, Margaret told herself firmly, but she knew that she would always believe that the ghosts of Priam's Priory had joined forces to stand guard over the old stones, frightening away the flesh-and-blood person who started for her in the passage.

Margaret went from the kitchen through the pantry and the dining room, and finally to the entrance to the priory room. She found David at the foot of the short steps to his room with his hand on the knob. She couldn't tell if he was arriving or departing.

"Ah, Margaret. What are you doing up at this hour? I couldn't sleep, so I thought I'd come down here. I find this room relaxing. The history of our family is centered right here. Don't you get a sense of the distant past, the monks assembled and saying their prayers and wondering what the nuns on the other side of the establishment are doing?"

"Where did you come from?"

"Why, my rooms."

"Were you alone?"

"Certainly!" He sounded indignant. "I told you how matters stood between me and Chloe."

"Did you hear any sounds from Roach's room? Or Jazmin's? Any comings or goings from the Indian wing? Did you see anyone roaming about upstairs or down? Were you in the Nun's Walk just now?"

"No, of course not. Everyone's asleep. What is this all about?"

"I have just seen the murderer in the Nun's Walk, leaving behind the rifle that must have killed Nigel. Whoever it was must have come through the door here. I didn't touch the rifle, but that's what it must be. Better than trying to hide it, don't you think? Leave it somewhere to be found by the police, and no one knows where it had been concealed or by whom."

"I'm sure I don't know what you're getting at," David said.

"I'm getting at asking you to tell me that it wasn't you."

He almost laughed. "Don't be ridiculous. I am a titled gentleman farmer, not a murderer."

"Wally knew whoever it was, even if it was pretending to be a ghost. He behaved as though it was a friend." She decided not to tell him about what else she thought she saw. He would think she was going crazy, seeing ghosts everywhere.

"Wally always hopes for the best. Ought you not get along to bed?"

Margaret wished that she could knock on De Vere's door, waken him, and tell him what had happened, but she knew what he would say: "Phone the police and let them handle it."

Instead, she said to her brother, "I want you to come with me while I telephone to the police about the rifle."

She had no idea whether Westron was staying in the vicinity, but perhaps the village constable's wife had found room for him in their house. She couldn't allow the rifle to lie unattended in the Nun's Walk until morning.

While David waited in the Great Hall, Margaret went to the telephone in the alcove and dialed the constable's number.

"Lady Margaret!" She whirled around, startled. Harbert had appeared at the end of the hallway, wearing a distinguished robe of some heavy, dark fabric. He seemed unsettled by the sight of her.

"I have to make a call," Margaret said. "I didn't mean to waken anyone."

"I haven't slept well since the troubles began," Harbert said. He was looking at her curiously. "Is anything wrong?"

"No, go back to bed. It's all right," she said. "The ghosts are about to look after me."

"Surely not," Harbert said uneasily. "I mean to say, if the staff gets to hear of it—"

"David is also watching over me," she said, and raised

her hand to forestall further talk as the sleepy voice of the constable came on the line.

"So sorry to wake you," Margaret said, "but I've found something I felt the police should know about right away. . . . "

Margaret and David returned to the Nun's Walk and waited at the far end to see that no one appeared to remove the rifle until the police came.

Chapter 18

Of course, Harbert had had to stay up to let the police in. Of course, Mrs. Domby had felt it necessary to appear with her hair done up in a remarkable frilled nightcap in order to keep her eye on everything. Margaret had her own reasons for staying until Westron appeared from somewhere, rather cross and sleepy-eyed. He retrieved the rifle and heard Margaret's tale, listened doubtfully to David's reasons for being near the priory room, and departed into the night. An uneasy peace descended again on the Priory.

Still, when Margaret rose somewhat late the next morning after what seemed like little sleep, matters were not serene in the household. She heard Harbert's voice raised in an unseemly manner from the pantry. A door slammed. The sharp tones of Mrs. Domby reached her. Roach was again shouting into the telephone, cajoling and haranguing and doing deals.

In the dining room, she came upon a disconsolate Chloe Waters picking at streaky bacon and eggs. Mrs. Domby had sublimated her anxieties by preparing far too much food. A sideboard of breakfast dishes slowly cooled and congealed— eggs and bacon, sausages, porridge, fried mushrooms and grilled tomatoes, toast in silver toast racks, even a plate of kippers. Her larder must be definitively depleted now. A sniffling Tilda collected plates that had been emptied by earlier breakfasters. Perhaps the sturdy village girl had been the one to feel the force of Harbert's ill temper.

"What *is* going on?" Chloe said plaintively. "David will scarcely speak to me. He said the murderer was about in the night shooting at you, and the police had been here, and then he went off."

"No one shot at me," Margaret said, "but someone who might have been the murderer was roaming around here." She turned her attention to toast and marmalade (the real thing, thank you, Mrs. Domby). She was growing tired of Chloe's whining, and happily, she decided to take her ill temper elsewhere, just as De Vere found his way to the dining room and gazed about at the portraits and the laden sideboard. He looked far better rested than she felt.

"Have some breakfast," Margaret said. "There seems to be just about anything your heart desires. We usually don't have this much for the beginning of a hard day of hunting. You'd better sit down while I tell you what went on last night."

While De Vere tucked into a large plate of eggs, bangers, and bacon, with a few tomatoes on the side, she explained.

"I don't like it," he said. "You are supposed to stick with me."

"You were there in spirit," Margaret said. "Your name scared my *faux* ghost away."

"It was probably the mention of a gun," De Vere said. "This has got to stop."

"We'll go to the fair today, and forget the murders," she said cheerfully, and knew that she wouldn't. She'd spend the day looking over her shoulder to see who was behind her. "You'll get a glimpse of village life in the raw, and then we'll have a plowman's lunch at the pub. We can slip away quietly, and forgo Mrs. Domby's hearty midday meal, although she does do a nice roast beef on a Sunday. And you'll discover at the fair that I am super at the coconut shy." When De Vere cocked his head in bemusement, she explained patiently, "You throw coconuts at other ones set up in a row. When you knock one down, you win a prize."

"And what do you win?"

"A coconut, of course."

De Vere looked more puzzled. "What do you do with it?"

"Nothing. It's the winning that counts."

He chuckled. "I hate to dampen your enthusiasm by reminding you that there's a basket of coconuts in every bodega in Manhattan, and probably every Food Emporium and Gristide's as well. You can acquire one readily by picking it up and paying the modest price."

"One forgets," Margaret said. "They seemed so exotic when I was a child. They always have dodgems, too."

"Those cars that bump into each other? We had those in Jersey when I was a kid. I was pretty good. I'll take you on."

"A challenge," Margaret said. "I'll tell Mrs. Domby not to expect us to lunch."

In the kitchen, she found no delicious smells of a traditional English lunch.

Mrs. Domby said, "As soon as Tilda clears the dining room and the washing up is finished, I'm off to the fair. Mr. Harbert will drive me. There's nothing decent in the house for a good meal, so his lordship has advised the film people to take themselves off to the pub. The Indians can fend for themselves. I'm sure I'm too upset by everything to do a proper lunch." She pushed back a strand of red hair from her forehead. The efforts of breakfast seemed to have exhausted her.

"Is David about?"

"He went to the village not ten minutes ago," Mrs. Domby said. "He drove off with Miss Waters."

"He was probably recruited by the vicar to appear at the fair," Margaret said. "We'll catch up with him. I don't suppose you've seen Doris about today."

Mrs. Domby drew herself up. "Lady Margaret, I am not accustomed to being treated like an underservant. I bear a great many responsibilities in this house, and I hope I give satisfaction."

"She was at you, I take it."

"Demanded in no uncertain terms that a very substantial breakfast be brought up to her room immediately; the tea Tilda took up wasn't sufficient. I explained that things were at sixes and sevens and there was plenty of breakfast set out in the dining room. Harbert finally took something up, but she wouldn't let him in. He had to leave it on a tray on the floor outside her door. I wonder who she thinks she is. Those royal airs don't mean a thing to me, although I'm sure I try to treat her as well as any guest who ever stayed here. . . . ''

"She's nervous," Margaret said soothingly. Harbert appeared from the pantry, in ordinary country clothes, the better to blend into the fair. "We're all on edge."

De Vere had made himself at home in the Great Hall. He seemed to like the idea of being able to choose from a variety of places to wander.

"Come along," she said. "I'll drive."

The mild debate that followed finally convinced De Vere that she knew better than he which was the correct side of the road, especially given the narrow lanes that led to the village. Then the maharajah's old servant was at their side, bowing low with his palms together before his face. De Vere took in the sight of him with equanimity.

"He seems to want something of us," he said. The servant made a waving gesture toward the house. "In fact, he seems to want us to follow him."

"Sir, madam, please to attend His Highness," the servant said in perfectly good English. "He is desiring to receive sir and madam in his rooms."

Margaret shrugged. "We'd better take the opportunity, since Ram-Sam is especially difficult to see these days. You will find the experience interesting."

The servant opened the door to the maharajah's suite with a flourish and bowed them in. If anything, the drawing room had become more Indian and less English since Margaret's recent visit. The curtains were closed, and in lieu of electric light, a number of thick candles had been lighted. The scent of incense was very strong. Pictures of Ganesh, the Hindu elephant god, now decorated one wall, and various other deities of his religion adorned others. Several vases were filled with a profusion of bright yellow marigolds plundered from the Priory cutting gardens. Margaret even thought she heard the faint sound of a sitar drifting in from the dressing room. A recording surely, but it contributed to the atmosphere.

The Maharajah of Tharpur had donned tight white leggings and a high-collared cream brocade jacket that reached almost to his knees. Around his neck was a triple strand of black pearls, and on his head he wore a squarish cap with a large gold brooch heavily studded with mammoth diamonds. He was sitting cross-legged on a sofa that was piled with red cushions.

"Highness," Margaret said, mystified by the transformation, "how good of you to receive us." She sensed that he was not in a jovial mood today. "May I present Mr. De Vere from New York."

The maharajah nodded gravely.

De Vere glanced at Margaret, and said, "It's an honor to meet you, sir." The maharajah seemed to find that acceptable, and nodded.

There was silence for a moment, then the old servant tottered in with small cups of dark tea. The maharajah gestured for them to sit, so they sat on the edge of two straight-backed chairs.

"I wished to say farewell to you," the maharajah said. "I have decided to move on. I shall go to Claridge's, which I have always found most comfortable and accommodating. Yes?"

"Yes, certainly it is," Margaret said. "Have the police given you permission to leave?"

The maharajah said, "I have consented to receive a gentleman from the police today, to proclaim my innocence."

That interview seemed to explain the maharajah's sudden immersion in the splendors of the raj: he had done it to impress the authorities, although Margaret wasn't sure that Westron would be awed into allowing His Highness his way.

"My servants will commence packing to be ready to depart at any moment," he said. "The official permission is soon to come."

"And Doris?"

"Doris is of no concern now," he said. He waved his hand

as though to dismiss all thoughts of Doris, and the gems in the rings on his plump fingers caught the light from the candles. "She has been, I think, disloyal to me. Although I have done much for her, she wants more. She has gone so far as to appropriate objects of great value to me. I do not worry about money, but there are things that are relating to my traditions that she does not understand. She sees only the thing itself and not the essence of the thing. If we were in India," he said solemnly, "I would throw her to the crocodiles."

Margaret and De Vere looked at each other, and then the maharajah laughed. "Of course, I would not do such a thing. It is a figure of speech, as I was taught in your fine English school, Eton. Did you know I was being taught there as a boy? Not for long, because I had to return to Tharpur when my grandfather was dying and I was soon to become ruler of my state. With the permission of the British, of course."

He reached out to the table at his side and picked up a thick album. "Before I leave," he said, "I should like to show you and your gentleman how life was in those days when we still ruled a kingdom. Come, come, move your chairs."

To Margaret's surprise, De Vere obeyed promptly, and the three of them gazed upon faded, yellowing photographs of a way of life long vanished.

"This is my grandfather, from whom I inherited the ruling powers of Tharpur. He is seated on the *gaddi*, the chair we called our throne, receiving the British political agent. And here he is coming in from the royal *shikar*, the tiger hunt, with three tigers—all of them over eight feet."

De Vere seemed entranced by the pages and pages of photos.

"Here is my wedding procession. Look at our elephants—they are gone now—and the crowds of my subjects celebrating. Here is Her Highness in her wedding clothes." The late maharani was a tiny thing, totally swathed from head to toe in heavy garments so that no bit of her was visible. "And this is the private *durbar* room in the city palace, where I would hold audiences with my ministers of state. A beautiful room, but now we cannot keep it so well. Since Her Highness is no longer alive, I believe I shall turn the palace into a hotel, the way Udaipur and Jaipur have done, and bring the tourists to Tharpur. Ah, here is your uncle Lawrence, Margaret, as a young man.''

Margaret peered at the stiffly posed group of young sustainers of the empire, and picked out her uncle in a thick suit and tropical topee beside the young maharajah in brocade and turban.

"Uncle Lawrence will be here tomorrow," she said.

"If I am still here, I shall be very, very pleased to see him again," the maharajah said. "Two old men will share our losses."

"Do you intend to leave before Mr. Roach has spent all the money you've invested in his film?"

The maharajah chuckled faintly. "Another one who steals from me. He is bilking me, oh yes, I know that. But happily, I can still afford to lose money to amuse myself. And it has provided the opportunity to make charming new acquaintances."

Margaret told herself to remind Jazmin Burns again of the rigors of everyday life in India, even for the well off.

The maharajah spoke a word in his native language, and the servant reappeared and opened the door. The audience was over.

"You cannot leave without a memento," His Highness said. He pointed to the little gilt box on the desk. It was the same box from which he had taken the emerald necklace intended for her worth thousands and thousands of pounds. She obediently went to the desk, and hesitated before she picked the box up and brought it to him.

"Only a modest trinket that even your old nanny would not deny you." He handed her a silver filigree ring set with tiny emeralds this time. Truly a trinket, she was relieved to see. "Please to take it, to please an old man."

"Thank you, Highness," Margaret said. "This I will accept."

The servant bowed them out the door.

"What was that all about?" De Vere asked as they went downstairs.

"Got up to impress the police, I think," Margaret said, "and us in passing. He told me something, perhaps without meaning to," she added thoughtfully. "The jewels and possessions he has left must surely be worth millions, since he started out with many times that." She looked at her ring, which just fit her smallest finger. "I wonder what Doris appropriated."

"I judge nothing significant," De Vere said. "That fellow takes good care of what he has, and doesn't leave about what he can't afford to lose."

Chapter 19

When they were at last under way toward the village and the fair, Margaret was determined to put aside all the facts and suspicions she had been accumulating and simply enjoy a peaceful time with De Vere.

This was not so readily done, since De Vere displayed a certain uneasiness about Margaret's carefree driving style as they flew along the country lanes entirely familiar to her but strange and dangerous to him.

"Watch out for the curve," De Vere said, and gripped the dashboard in mild panic.

"Don't you go careening through New York in those plain dark cars with lights flashing?" Margaret asked.

"I seldom have had occasion to do so," he said faintly.

Margaret rounded a curve between the high hedgerows without damaging them. "I remember once coming upon a large cow that had somehow managed to stray from one of the farms," Margaret said. "Slight damage to the hood of Daddy's car, none to the cow, although the farmer claimed she didn't give milk for a week. Ah, here are some people I want you to meet."

Phyllis and Lester Flood were trudging along the road's edge in single file toward the village. Lester had a number of expensive-looking cameras slung around his neck. From the slight limp that was detectable, Phyllis's high-heeled pumps were starting to pain her.

"Can we give you a lift?" Margaret called out.

"Oh, yes," Phyllis said, and almost sprinted toward the car. "Lester says that exercise in good country air is healthy; I say we have a perfectly good Jag parked in front of our so-called house, but he says we shouldn't show off our material goods in front of our neighbors. . . . "

Margaret did not mention that even in the countryside, Jaguars were not all that rare a sight. Instead she merely introduced De Vere as a friend from New York, and proceeded toward the village.

One of the ubiquitous motorbikes passed them, going toward the Priory from the village, and Margaret said, "Another of the press hot on the Priory murders. I do wish they'd leave us alone."

She brought the car to a stop on the verge of the green. "I say, there's David doing his duty as the Earl of Brayfield."

David was watching the warm-up for a cricket match, with Chloe clinging to his shadow. Across the way, surrounded by a cluster of admirers, Lys was standing in the doorway of the Riming Man. She looked fetching in her tight jeans and sexy shirt. The fair at the other end of the green was in full swing, with the *pum-pum-pum* of the steam calliope keeping time with the up and down of the merry-go-round horses. The freshly painted red and gold circus wagons with Victorian curlicues and gingerbread trim formed a backdrop to the array of booths with rifle targets, ring tosses, and other games of skill. The prized stuffed animals were piled high, and the cotton candy man was busily serving pure pink spun sugar to the village children. Meanwhile other children were being whirled into oblivion by a ride that spun them around in baskets at the end of thin chains. Ladies of the parish were selling preserves and cakes at a long table while packs of frisky dogs frolicked about the green, watched over by benevolent little old ladies and brisk country squires.

"Quaint, what?" Margaret said.

"Aw, we had carnivals like this back in Ohio. I even brought them in to set up near some of my malls. Made a fortune,'' Lester said, then added, ''Another fortune. I think I'll have a word with Lord Brayfield. Nigel left some unfinished business. Phyl, you go along with Lady Margaret.''

"I'd rather walk about on my own,'' Phyllis said. "Margaret and her friend probably have things to talk about.''

"Why don't we all meet at the pub?'' Margaret said, feeling warmly grateful toward Phyllis.

"I spy the dodgems,'' De Vere said. "I'll show you driving like you've never seen.'' He took her arm and hurried her away from the Floods.

"I mentioned Nigel's apparent taste for blackmail and other financial undertakings,'' Margaret said. "I wonder if that has anything to do with Lester's need to speak to David.''

"Murder, blackmail, ghosts, deluded princes, petulant wives, glamorous movie stars, crooked producers.'' De Vere shook his head as he guided her toward the ride, which was well populated by determined drivers bouncing off chunky beetlelike vehicles inside a pavilion with a low fence surrounding it. "I can see that the England I imagined is not . . . what I imagined. Here, you pick out the right money.''

"This is a pound coin,'' Margaret said. "And this is fifty pence.'' Then they were into their cars and into the boisterous crowd.

Pum-pum-pum went the calliope, *pop-pop* went the little rifles aimed at red and green ducks in a row. Margaret bounced off a car driven by the son of the village postmistress and spun around so that she was facing the fence rather than center of the ring, where De Vere in a red car was backing up and turning so as to pursue her.

She was startled to see through the slats of the fence around the dodgem ride the maharajah's old turbaned servant proceeding through the throng, trailed by three Indian ladies in saris, their faces modestly covered by the edges of the filmy veils they wore over their heads. They stopped at the booths and chattered and pointed. They must have walked over the meadows to reach the fair instead of using the road. The fairgoers paid them no heed. Perhaps they thought they were part of the show. On the other hand, England had grown accustomed to seeing Indians of all sorts, even if they were not all that common in the countryside.

Margaret raised herself from the dodgem's seat to look over the top of the fence. Now she could see four Indian ladies instead of three. The one hanging back behind the others was quite a bit taller, and held the edge of the scarf over her head so that her face was covered. Could it be Doris? Margaret had no idea how many servants the maharajah had with him, but her suspicions grew stronger as the taller woman separated herself from the others and edged away toward the long booth that housed a penny arcade filled with old-fashioned slot machines and games. She paused between the penny arcade and the bright red house on wheels next to it, and looked back at the fairgoers. Then she slipped between the two and was gone. Margaret saw that she had a woven bag of many colors slung over her shoulder. The turbaned servant and his three other charges seemed not even to have noticed her presence. They were at a booth trying to roll little black balls into slots to win a small box of sweets.

Margaret's car was rammed from behind by De Vere. She pressed her accelerator and spun the wheel, turning the car toward De Vere, who laughed and evaded her. She wished the ride would end so that she could find out why Doris had decided to honor the fair with her presence.

As soon as the power died to end the ride, Margaret leapt from her car and hastened to the ramp. The presumed Doris was now nowhere to be seen.

"Doris is here. We've got to find her," Margaret said, and grabbed De Vere's hand.

David had disappeared, although Mrs. Domby could be seen inspecting the preserves table.

"I don't see the once and future Mrs. Tharpur anywhere," De Vere said, "but behold the beauteous Jazmin Burns, with your maharajah."

True enough, His Highness, wearing his fancy royal costume, was escorting Jazmin through the fair.

"And with them," Margaret said, "is the less attractive Quintus Roach."

The citizens of Upper Rime paid a bit more attention to

Jazmin and the maharajah than they had to the maharajah's servant. Perhaps some of them did keep current on who was really, *really* hot in Hollywood. Roach made a pointed effort to clear a path for them to the merry-go-round, just as Phyllis Flood descended from a shiny black steed and was snapped in the act by Lester's high-tech Japanese camera. In the pause between tunes on the calliope, one of the motorbikes parked near the pub started with a roar, as an intrepid journalist went in search of yet another lurid tale from Upper Rime to titillate the British public. Harbert had now condescended to appear at Mrs. Domby's side to carry her purchases of homemade jellies and cakes. There was a shout from spectators who had gathered to watch the cricket match: the local side's star batsman had hit one for six.

Margaret threaded her way through the crowd to the penny arcade booth. A girl was selling the big old-fashioned pennies, now long obsolete, needed to operate the antique machines. Margaret paused at the side of the booth, and then went behind it, half afraid of what she would find. Another dead person would be too much.

She found nothing. The grass was overgrown under the trees behind the wagons, and a faint dirt track led off to the cricket pitch and the pub. If it had been Doris she had seen, Doris was now gone, leaving no evidence that she had been there. But gone where?

De Vere caught up with her, and found her deep in thought.

"Nothing," Margaret said.

"Did you expect to find another body?"

She looked at him. "Now that you mention it, yes. I thought Doris was meeting someone she couldn't be seen with at the house. I thought she might be trying her own hand at blackmail, only to be silenced like the others. Maybe I've had a wrong suspicion all along. Let's go over to the pub."

When they emerged from behind the booth and wagons, they came face-to-face with Quintus Roach. "Mr. Roach," Margaret said, "I thought you would be preparing to film." She continued to scan the crowd, but Doris was not in sight.

"No good," Roach said. He eyed De Vere. "You're the

New York cop they've been talking about. Quintus Roach.''
He forced De Vere into a hearty handshake. "You ought to
feel right at home with all these murders. See, Lady Margaret, these guys I'm in this production with, they're in New
York, and there's some Japanese money involved, but that's
true of everything nowadays. Anyhow, they don't want me
to go ahead with filming here until these murders get straight-
ened out. Bad publicity, they say, and I say any publicity is
good publicity, but if you're dealing with people who aren't
in the business, they don't understand. I'm sending the crew
on today to the next location, and I'm leaving as soon as the
cops say I can. I mean, I didn't murder anybody, so why
keep me? All I got to do is keep Jazmin. She has a contract,
but she seems to think . . .'' He shrugged. "It'll be her
funeral, know what I mean?''

"Yes,'' Margaret said, "in a manner of speaking, I do.''
She frowned at a very obvious thought that had come to her.
There was no Doris in her sari, because Doris had managed
to change her clothes. Slacks beneath the sweeping fabric, a
shirt tucked in her bag to slip on over the bodice worn under
the sari, and Doris became an ordinary fairgoer.

Her brother had reappeared to continue playing Lord of
the Land, chatting with old ladies and patting infants in their
mother's arms. Chloe was not in evidence, but Lys had abandoned her post at the pub, and was walking with David,
looking amused by his stately progress through the crowd.

"Excuse us, Mr. Roach. I need to speak to David.''

Margaret pursued her brother in the direction of the pub,
with De Vere on her heels.

As she passed the cricket match in progress, she said, "I'd
explain, but we don't have time. . . . ''

"I know the game,'' De Vere said. "You'd be surprised
how many cricket matches take place around New York. The
West Indians are very keen on it, and policemen often find
themselves in Mount Vernon or Queens or Brooklyn on
pleasant summer afternoons just when the local eleven has
its innings.''

"Oh goodness!'' Margaret said suddenly. The batsman

had just been bowled, but it was not this that had prompted her words.

"Sam, I have to get back to the Priory at once. Before the film crew leaves for their next location. They have two big caravans. House trailers." She headed toward her car.

"What now?" De Vere called after her, and then followed.

"Doris," she said. "I've just figured it out. She's making a break for freedom—possibly escaping from a person who might decide to silence her, and just as possibly making off with some little object of incalculable value that will take care of her for life. If she lives."

De Vere held on as they careened down the lanes toward Priam's Priory.

Fortunately, when they came upon the first caravan, lumbering slowly away from the house, Margaret managed to brake in time to stop just before they smashed.

"So sorry, Geoff," she said when Roach's director of photography jumped down from the driver's seat. "I'm glad I caught you." The second caravan was right behind the first. "Could I speak to your passenger?"

Geoff scratched his head. "How'd you know?" he asked. "It was supposed to be top secret."

"I guessed," Margaret said. "Is she in this caravan or the next?"

"In this one." He jerked his head toward his vehicle.

De Vere said, "I underestimate you, Margaret. You do make a pretty good detective."

Margaret opened the door into the trailer and peered in.

"Oh, damn!" Chloe Waters said petulantly. "I thought I'd get away."

"Chloe!" Margaret said. "Whatever are you doing?"

"I couldn't bear it any longer. The police and the press, and David behaving as though I weren't there. I had to get away. This person—" she indicated Geoff with her chin "—promised he'd drop me at a station down the line, where I could catch a train to London. No one was supposed to know, and since I absolutely didn't murder anybody, the police will forget about me, don't you think? Daddy was going to pick me up at my flat in Sloane Square, and I'd fly out tonight for the continent. He has that condominium on the coast of Spain, and I could stay there for ages and ages.''

Margaret put her head in her hands.

"A pretty good detective," De Vere said, "but not a great one, not yet."

"Do I have to go back?" Chloe said tearfully.

"Oh, I don't care," Margaret said. She had no interest in what Chloe did.

"Super!" Chloe said.

"You don't have someone else hidden in the next caravan, do you?" Margaret asked Geoff hopefully.

"No one. Swear to that. Just my mate driving and the wardrobe girl."

"There!" Chloe said, tasting freedom and possibly the good red wines of Spain. "Drive on, Geoffrey!"

"The lady has to back up so I can get by," Geoff said. Then he added in a low voice to Margaret, "This isn't going to get me in trouble with the coppers, is it?"

"Probably," Margaret said, "but not a lot."

She didn't speak to De Vere as she backed up until she could pull off the road. The caravans proceeded past, and she thought she caught sight of Chloe's delicate little hand waving happily from one of the windows.

"Margaret," De Vere said, "my advice would be to inform your policeman about what you know or think about Doris, and let him handle matters."

Margaret sighed. "All right," she said slowly. "I will."

Chapter 20

Priam's Priory was virtually empty.

There was no response to repeated knocks on Doris's door, but Margaret had not expected to find her there. The maharajah was still at the fair, along with his entire entourage. The Priory's servants seemed to have vanished, and even Westron had cleared out of the library.

Margaret stood at the foot of the principal staircase and scowled. "If Doris is dead, where does the body repose?"

"If you saw her at the fair, and you didn't then find her body there, you have to assume she's alive until you have evidence that she isn't. She's probably somewhere about the village," De Vere said.

Margaret shook her head. "She isn't. If she's not dead, she's got away, and I don't know how she managed it. She's on the run, Sam, because I think she knows who the murderer is."

"You're sure she's not the murderer?"

"When it was just the maharani, she seemed the obvious suspect. Rather too obvious. But she was so plainly frightened after Nigel died. Then I started thinking about who else—"

"Tell Westron. And I hate to mention it, but I'm hungry."

"I forgot about going to the pub for lunch," Margaret said. "Let's find something here."

The refrigerator in the spotless kitchen was rather bare.

"Here's a bit of ham in the fridge, and some cheese," Margaret said. "Mrs. Domby is down to her last crumbs. Good thing the larder will be restocked tomorrow. Three quarters of a bottle of white Bordeaux. Half a loaf of bread. Let's eat in the garden. Look, could you take these things outside? Right through the little gate. I want to telephone first."

She sent him out to the nodding roses and sweet peas and buzzing honeybees and went back to the hallway outside the Great Hall.

When she dialed the constable's number, it rang repeatedly. She was about to give up when the constable's wife answered.

"So sorry to disturb you. Is the constable about?" Margaret asked.

"Not here," she told Margaret. "He's off with the men from Scotland Yard."

"As soon as he returns, please ask him or Mr. Westron to call Lady Margaret? Thank you so much." She replaced the receiver and turned. "Ah!" The sight of Harbert in the entrance startled her.

"Back from the fair, m'lady," Mrs. Domby said cheerfully behind him. "Old Mrs. Penge made some of her lovely ginger preserve; so hard to find it made right nowadays." Mrs. Domby bustled in. "Mr. Harbert, if you'll just put those things in the kitchen. Did you catch a sight of those Indian ladies at the fair? I couldn't believe my eyes. They never set foot out of the house. And didn't His Highness look like a million pounds in that outfit. The vicar was saying how pleased he was to receive a donation from Mr. Flood for the church roof."

"Did you see Doris at the fair?" Margaret asked. She looked from one to the other. "I thought I caught sight of her."

"Her High and Mighty Highness said she was keeping to her room," Mrs. Domby said. Harbert shook his head.

"She seems to have gone missing," Margaret said. "Mrs. Domby, Mr. De Vere and I took a few bits of this and that from the fridge. I hope you don't mind. And we'll dine out this evening at that little place on the road to Cotterpynne that used to be so good.''

"His lordship says it's keeping up to snuff," Mrs. Domby said. "And the larder will be full again tomorrow, don't you worry. His lordship was starting back when we left the fair. He wants to see you in a bit, he said.''

Margaret found De Vere dozing peacefully in the walled garden, having eaten his share of their meager lunch. Rather than wake him, she walked about inspecting the flowers, and thinking about Doris. How had she managed to get away from Upper Rime? No answer came immediately, so she nudged De Vere with a toe.

De Vere opened one eye. "One day out of New York and I've turned into a man of leisure. I hope my spirit isn't broken for good.''

"That will never happen," Margaret said. "It's just this fabulous country air, to quote Jazmin Burns. I want to have a chat with my brother, and later Mrs. Domby will give us a proper tea, and later still you'll take me out to dinner at a lovely, romantic place on a little river a few miles away where we can eat on the deck and watch people punting. Endless hours of amusement planned for the kiddies.''

"I could grow accustomed to this life," De Vere said. "Nothing but lazing around in the sun.''

"Sun doesn't always shine," Margaret said, "and we're off to London in the morning.''

David sat in his favorite chair, looking depressed.

"Cheer up, David," Margaret said. "Chloe's gone. If she's the murderer, I've let her get away scot-free. If she's not, she won't darken your doors by intention.''

David managed to look grateful. Margaret had handled another problem for him.

"Of course, you still have a problem. Absolutely everyone remains a suspect except me," Margaret said.

"Westron seems to have been superseded by two grim men who don't care a bit about being diplomatic. They give the impression of believing we should all be locked up, starting with Ram-Sam and ending up with Tilda. Well, perhaps not you," David said.

"I hope not, since I plan to drive down to London in the morning to fetch Uncle Lawrence. De Vere will come with me, in case the murderer pursues me thinking I needed to be silenced."

"I don't picture any of us with a bloody dagger or aiming a rifle at old Nigel, impossible though he was. I still say it must have been someone from the outside, in both cases."

"In a sense," Margaret said.

"I believe that once everyone clears out, I shan't have any more guests at the Priory," David said. "Too much trouble, and I can't spare the time. I've got to take care of the financial mess, especially now that Roach is clearing out and paying only part of the fees we'd agreed on. These other arrangements are going to take time."

"Exactly how much of the Priory lands do you plan to sell to Flood?"

David looked guilty. "Not much. Not the polo field. We're talking about some farmland beyond the woods. It's never produced properly, and old Wilf is getting too old to farm anyhow. Flood has suggested we put in a minimall with multiplex cinemas." David said the words as though he wasn't quite sure what they meant.

"No!"

"Rather the way I feel."

"It diminishes the inheritance," Margaret said, "assuming you do intend eventually to marry one of the Chloe Waters of this world and produce offspring."

"I do intend to marry," David said. "All in good time. I say, when you're in London, would you stop somewhere and buy a sort of nice thing?"

"Thing?"

"Something a girl would like."

"Girl. A little girl, a big girl, or a young woman of taste and refinement?"

"Taste and refinement," David murmured. "Grown-up. You must know what I mean."

"Nothing too intimate, nothing too terribly impersonal. Not something satin with touches of lace, but not a book."

"Exactly."

"What size would you say?"

David thought. "About Lys's size. Look, I've got to see one of the farmers who has a problem. Agriculture has gone to hell in this country."

"I'll find something," Margaret said.

"There's one thing I forgot to mention about Doris," David said as he stood up.

"May be too late," Margaret said. "Doris has scarpered as well, although at this point, I can't say what sort of reward she's gone to. What about her?"

"She never actually told me so, but I had the impression that she'd been married."

Margaret sighed. Another piece fell into place. "I rather thought that might be the case." She didn't add that this would likely have displeased His Highness enormously if he were told of it by a trusted family member. A displeased Highness might see to it that one was cast out into the world, and one's only defense would be to acquire enough things of value to take care of oneself, and then to disappear. Doris had managed to disappear.

"It came to me when I was thinking about marriage," David said. "Just today, actually. Doris said once she'd next marry for money, because marrying for love was stupid. Something like that. Margaret, are you listening?"

"Closely," she said. "A pity she didn't manage to marry the maharajah in fact as well as in fiction to enjoy the wealth he still has. Well, perhaps she thinks she has something to enjoy, even without him."

"And now Jazmin will reap all benefits."

"Jazmin," Margaret said, "will take the money and run, if I am not mistaken."

"Things were much simpler when I was a boy," said David. "They are still at it, by the way." He held up another London tabloid. The headline promised "Startling New Revelations: Murder at the Priory." Priam's Priory was becoming a veritable cottage industry for the popular press.

Margaret sat down suddenly. New revelations. She had an answer to Doris's escape, and if she was not mistaken, even more startling revelations would be conveyed to the press in very short order.

"De Vere and I are dining out tonight," she said, "and I'm off to London in the morning. We'll talk when I get back." She hurried to the telephone, and called the Riming Man.

Yes, Lys told her, several of the press boys had gone back to London that afternoon. No, she didn't know if any had picked up a passenger, but she could ask the one or two who still remained.

"See what you can discover, please," Margaret said, and waited.

Lys came back on the line. "Somebody thought that one of the reporters with a motorbike had a female passenger when he left. Tallish, blondish. I think I caught sight of someone like that at the bar, clutching a big bright bag like it was holding the Crown Jewels, but she's not here now."

"Lovely," Margaret said. "Just what I wanted to know."

Doris had not only enlisted the aid of the press for her departure, but she had taken a leaf from Nigel's book. A promise to tell the absolute inside story on the Priory murders, for a price. She'd managed a way to run from danger, and get paid for it. Clever Doris!

Margaret stopped in the kitchen to speak to Mrs. Domby, who was doing some washing up, although Margaret couldn't imagine where the pile of dishes had come from.

"Ah, Lady Margaret, didn't you startle me. I'm expecting to turn around and see a ghost at any second."

"Doesn't David give you help for the kitchen?"

"I couldn't bear to have a chattering girl about. I've been upset about all this murder business. The maharani dying was bad enough." She looked a trifle guilty. "Excuse me for thinking that His Highness might just have decided to get her out of his hair, and it wasn't any of my business. Foreigners have their way of dealing with domestic problems."

She ran a wet cloth over a countertop and then repeated it again and yet again, although there was not a speck of dirt to be seen. "Mr. Nigel was a different story. Knew him from a boy, and he was as sweet as could be to me. Never forgot to bring me a little present."

"His father will be here tomorrow. Rooms are at a premium, but Miss Waters departed suddenly. Uncle Lawrence can have her room."

"Gone, is she?" The news seemed to cheer her immensely. "I can't help but admit that I heard one or two sharp words between her and his lordship. Didn't sound promising for a happy life together." She sniffed, and the implication was clear: Miss Chloe Waters transformed into the Countess of Brayfield at the village church with a pack of angelic children in attendance would spell the end of Mrs. Domby's long service at the Priory. "Don't you worry, Lady Margaret. I'll see to Mr. Lawrence."

"Excellent," Margaret said. "And if I am not mistaken, Doris has gone off to London as well."

Mrs. Domby suddenly became very busy, placing cups on a tea tray, folding linen napkins and refolding them, rearranging the silver teapot and the hot water jug.

"She was no better than she should be, if you ask me, and that is excluding whatever business she was involved in with His Highness," Mrs. Domby said. "Whispering around with Mr. Nigel like they were sweethearts. She always looked too bold."

"You've seen Doris before this visit?"

"I might remember seeing a snap of her Mr. Nigel showed me, taken at his father's house. Nice little place Mr. Lawrence has in Surrey."

"I see," Margaret said. "Be sure that everyone knows that I've gone to London to fetch Uncle Lawrence so everything will be ready when he arrives. I will be meeting him at Harrods at one o'clock. I'll stop here before I leave to see about your order. I always like to roam through the Food Halls." Then she added a lie of which her old nanny would not have approved: "I think I shall leave Mr. De Vere behind, since it is just a quick trip."

"I'll be sending Potts down very early," Mrs. Domby said, "but I do forget things nowadays, and then it's too late. I used to go with him, and we'd go about to all the different shops, but it tires me so, and I can't trust any of the girls to know what's good and what isn't. Why, they barely learn to boil water these days. It's all these microwaves and packaged food."

Margaret felt she had done what she could to test her suspicions. Now she could go back to De Vere. He was gone from the garden, but had found the morning room, a small and cozy place with a nice view. He had picked out a few books and magazines from the library, and now was stretched out in an armchair with his feet up. Wally had determined that De Vere was a friend of the house, and had collapsed at his side.

"I'd love to have you see one of our ghosts," Margaret said, "but one can't summon them up on demand. I can only show you what exists in the here and now. Tomorrow it'll be bits of London. And Uncle Lawrence. An interesting man. Saw the end of the British Empire without turning a hair."

The day was beginning to draw to a close, although twilight was still a couple of hours away. The shadows were starting to lengthen across the thick lawns. It had remained fair throughout the day—Quintus Roach had canceled his filming at just the wrong time.

Then she saw Roach himself far out at the end of the lawn with Jazmin, their heads together as though they were plotting. The pageant before Margaret now began in earnest, as the maharajah himself made his stately way across the grass, trailed by the old servant and the three servant ladies in their brilliant saris. Jazmin saw him, and glided across the lawn with her arms outstretched.

"Oh, *really*," Margaret said half-aloud. "Just don't go packing your Louis Vuitton cases until you read up on the summer temperatures in the Indian desert."

Far away in the house, the telephone rang. Margaret tensed, and expected to be called to speak to Westron or the constable, but no summons came.

"It's time for another meal, and then another," Margaret said.

De Vere smiled. "I'm thinking of quitting the police," he said. "Murder in this setting is so free of the usual stress."

"We do keep a stiff upper lip," Margaret said. "I shall miss poor Nigel. He was only just my age."

The telephone rang again, and again Margaret was not called. If the police didn't care to hear what she thought, Margaret would do it her way.

Chapter 21

Margaret and De Vere were on the road to London early enough to get to the city in good time, but late enough to avoid the heaviest morning traffic. There was no discussion at all this time about who would drive. Margaret simply got into the driver's seat and they were off.

She noted that the Priory car used by the staff for errands about the countryside was gone. According to Mrs. Domby, who had a short list of items she wanted selected personally by Margaret, Potts had left for London early, carrying Harbert to the village, where he had some business. "I told Potts he might meet up with you at Harrods, but he has several places to stop for me and his lordship all about the city," she said.

"Lovely dinner last night, Sam," Margaret said, and tore down the double-lane highway past a lumbering lorry. "I ought to take you around to Runnymede, where the Magna Carta was signed. Next time." She whirled them through a traffic roundabout and braked at a red light.

"Yes, next time," De Vere said. He seemed to have grown accustomed to her carefree driving style.

Margaret accelerated rapidly when the light changed. "I had no idea you were such a skilled driver," he said. "Country lanes are one thing, but this is the big time."

"Americans think they invented driving," Margaret said. "Ah, here's that turn."

In spite of himself, De Vere tried to step on a brake pedal that existed only in his mind as Margaret rapidly turned left, then right again, and roared up a ramp to enter another multilane road packed with cars heading toward London, and lined with blank-faced reflecting office towers that could easily compete with any in Manhattan.

"So many changes," Margaret said. "This used to be country. But there's London up ahead. We'll park around Knightsbridge, I'll pick up my things at Harrods. Then we'll fetch Uncle Lawrence and perhaps drive about to see a few sights and head back."

"The truck!" De Vere said.

"What? Only a post office van. Don't worry. The queen hires very reliable people."

"What?"

"I'm joking, Sam. She doesn't do the hiring. Prince Charles does."

They reached Brompton Road without the deadly mishap De Vere had imagined.

"There's the Victoria and Albert," Margaret said. "A grand museum. You ought to see it. Next time. And Brompton Oratory, very impressive if you like lavish nineteenth-century churches in the baroque style. Now let's see about parking. I hate the parking garages, and they don't like transients on the streets around here. Ah, I remember there's a public car park in Beaufort Gardens, just a block or two from Harrods. Now, if we're lucky . . ."

They were lucky. Margaret turned in to a quiet oval lined with trees and cream-colored Edwardian buildings with iron balconies laden with boxes of red and white geraniums. The center of the cul-de-sac provided two rows of parallel parking, and just as they started to circle the oval, a car pulled out of a space. She paid her fee at the Pay and Display machine and stuck the ticket on the windshield.

De Vere's state of mind improved as soon as he found himself on the gray flagstone walk in front of a charming and discreet hotel that had been created out of one of the old houses. By the time she had guided him out of the cul-de-sac onto the pavement along Brompton Road, he seemed quite his normal self.

"That's Harrods just up ahead," Margaret said. The huge six-story terra-cotta building was outlined faintly in thousands of tiny white lights. "You would probably prefer to walk about rather than shop with me."

She was pleased to hear him say, "I hate shopping . . . but you're supposed to stick with me."

"We're miles away from the murders," she said. She didn't want him with her for the moment.

"I'll walk and look," he said. He eyed the thousands of tourists jamming the sidewalks, whose dollars were plumping up the British economy. A row of red and black London taxis was waiting in front of the store, and a green Harrods city tour bus was accepting passengers.

"If you head that way, you'll come to Sloane Street, and across from it, where Knightsbridge and Brompton divide, there's the Hyde Park Hotel. We used to stay there when I was a little girl. Daddy liked the rooms with views of Hyde Park. Why don't you meet Uncle Lawrence and me here—" she pointed to a flower stand on the corner of Hans Road across from Harrods "—in about an hour. Don't worry, I'll be fine." She hoped she would be.

She watched him stroll through the waves of tourists and disappear into the crowd. Then she walked with determination down Hans Road to the entrance to Harrods's confectionery department, where a short nearby escalator took her down to the order department.

"Madam?" A young man looked up from his computer.

"I'm inquiring whether Mr. Potts has picked up the order for Priam's Priory," Margaret said. "If not, I wish to purchase a few items to add to the packages. I am Lady Margaret Priam."

The young man punched a few keys and said, "The order is ready, but no one has yet called for it."

"Indeed," Margaret said, and looked around. No familiar

face was in view. ''Make another note, then, please. The order is not to be taken until I've made my additions.''

''Very good, m'lady.''

Margaret rode back upward to the Food Halls deep in thought. Her plan, such as it was, might be working.

She walked past the piles of boxed candies and cases filled with chocolates in the confectionery into the vegetable and fruit department, where the elaborate hanging light fixtures were monumental clusters of fruits, and then past the florist into the meat department. Along one wall was an array of game and poultry, and along the opposite wall were glass meat cases full of roasts and chops. She headed for the end of the room, where all manner of ham and bacon was sold. Mrs. Domby had apparently noted that De Vere liked his breakfast bacon and so felt a need for some backup rashers beyond what she had already ordered. As her purchase was being wrapped, she looked up at the Royal Doulton tile frieze of the hunt that circled the room beneath the barrel-shaped ceiling.

The store was crowded, but many of the shoppers were merely tourists, judging by the frequent flare of flashbulbs as photos recorded America's visit to the famous Harrods Food Halls. Margaret scanned the mobs. Once she thought she saw a familiar figure, but no. The person receiving a long green and white striped box of smoked salmon at the center case was no one she knew.

Mrs. Domby had specified a particular Stilton that she knew Uncle Lawrence was fond of, to be selected personally by Margaret from the cheese case, not one of the prepackaged varieties.

She entered an even busier room, with the long charcuterie cases along one side and the cheese along the other.

''Seventy-five . . . Seventy-six . . .'' The West Indian clerks behind the piles of salamis, sausages, and hams ready for slicing called out customers' numbers.

Halfway down the charcuterie counter, Margaret looked back over her shoulder and froze.

Harbert was standing next to the frozen foods display, near the opening leading from the fruits and vegetables room. He was scanning the faces of the shoppers as they passed him.

Now that she had actually seen him, and knew that he had either accompanied Potts or replaced him entirely in order to be here at Harrods, she felt a twinge of anxiety. She wanted to be sure, however, that he had come looking for her.

Margaret managed to insinuate herself between two customers at the charcuterie counter—a dotty-looking white-haired lady with a pince-nez and a floppy tan gardening hat, and a man wearing a proper dark pinstripe suit who ought to have been looking over stock prices in the City rather than examining Black Forest hams in Harrods.

Harbert walked past the frozen food cases toward the cheese and dairy section that ran the length of the opposite side of the room. Margaret moved in the same direction, on her side of the room, until she reached the pasta department. There, cheerful upper-class salesgirls packed up fresh pasta salads and cheese-stuffed croissants for Knightsbridge matrons. Margaret stood in the doorway that led to the bakery and pastry hall, and watched Harbert slowly moving in her direction, but he was not looking at the huge rounds of Camembert and Brie, the pots of mascarpone and containers of Devonshire cream. He was definitely searching for someone.

Nothing can happen in this big store, Margaret said to herself, and blinked as another tourist flashbulb exploded in her eyes.

"So sorry," she said hastily. "I do hope I didn't ruin your snapshot."

She would have preferred a confrontation of some sort at the Priory, with De Vere close at hand, but she had set the bait, and he had taken it. She was sure that Harbert believed that she knew whatever secrets he harbored, that she had learned them from Nigel or even Doris.

She ducked through the entrance to the next Food Hall, and found herself at the sweet-smelling *pâtisserie* counter. It was somewhat less crowded here, although the area where bread was sold had many shoppers. It was entered via a turnstile, and the only exits were the narrow aisles at each cash register. It was too much like a cul-de-sac. She could be trapped.

She hadn't been able to "ask Doris," as Nigel had said in his last words to her, but enough tantalizing hints made her start to realize that what she should have asked Doris was about Harbert.

The employee files in the estate office held no references about Richard Harbert from Sir Henry Blitworth. Indeed, there was no file at all for him. She recalled that Sir Henry had died not long ago, and had even rated an obituary in the *New York Times*, so there was no way of checking on a servant who might have forged his own references, thus making an assistant gamekeeper—surely a good shot with a rifle—into a proper butler.

It must have been Doris who had answered her call from New York in her Indian accent, teasing or taunting Harbert. From what she knew now of the Indian servants, they would not have dared to do such a thing. Doris must know Harbert rather better than it appeared.

If it had been Harbert who murdered two people at Priam's Priory, and he believed Margaret suspected him, how would he now attempt to rid himself of her? The shot by the lake had failed. Would it be another knife in the heart of a defenseless woman, this time in the middle of the crowds at Harrods? Or outside on Hans Road while the elegant row of brownstone houses looked on? Perhaps he would stalk her along Brompton Road and push her under the wheels of a speeding taxi. . . .

It was time to find Uncle Lawrence and De Vere and get away.

She looked cautiously over the heads of the shoppers, and her heart skipped as she spied Harbert as he peered into the big hall. She slipped past the ice cream department, back into the meat hall, and then past the floral arrangements on display into the narrow wine department. The aisles were crowded with people peering into bins of cheap Spanish reds. Older gentlemen were browsing at the rows of ports and Madeiras; young women were pondering whether to spend their pounds on a decent champagne for tonight's intimate dinner party.

Margaret stepped into the nearly empty fine jewelry department. She paused near the entrance and looked back. Harbert was solemnly pretending to examine a bin of Australian white wine.

Surely he knew where she was, but he was not closing in. What could he be waiting for?

She looked at her wristwatch. Uncle Lawrence would be waiting, and it was very nearly time to rendezvous with De Vere. She didn't want to leave either of them waiting too long.

She hurried for the Brompton Road side of the store, which would take her to the entrance to the escalator foyer. There she would find Uncle Lawrence, and perhaps some comforting security guards.

She was a little breathless when she reached the escalator lobby. Harbert was somewhere behind her, and there was Uncle Lawrence waiting patiently, clutching a green Harrods bag that must contain the new funeral tie for his son's last rites. A small suitcase lay at his feet.

With Uncle Lawrence was the last person she expected to see: Doris.

Now the three people who knew or suspected something about Harbert were together in one place. Did Harbert carry a gun? She wondered, as she grabbed the hands of Doris and her uncle and pulled them with her through the doors to Hans Road.

"Margaret, I say . . . look here."

"Trust me, Uncle Lawrence," Margaret said, "and don't you dare say one word, Doris, if you hope to come out of this undamaged."

Doris decided against arguing with Margaret.

They were quickly surrounded by the crowds on Brompton Road, and there was no sign of Harbert. It wouldn't be surprising, however, if he suddenly emerged from the store.

Her hope for safety in even larger numbers—the addition of De Vere—faded a bit. De Vere was nowhere to be seen.

"We need to get away from here for a bit," Margaret said. "Are you all right, Uncle Lawrence?"

He looked frailer than she remembered, and he was breathing a bit hard, but he seemed quite interested in what was happening.

"I don't understand," he said as he kept up with her pace, "but Nigel always said you were the cleverest one in the family—except for him. I suppose I must trust you."

"Where are we going?" Doris said. "I didn't bargain for this."

"Harbert is somewhere behind us, looking for me at least, and possibly Uncle Lawrence."

"And possibly me," Doris said, as Margaret took them along Brompton Road past the huge display windows.

"How would he know you'd be here?" Margaret took them down narrow streets and came to rest in Hans Place, a circle of buildings surrounding a patch of trees in the center. The road around Hans Place was packed with parked cars, but there were very few people in evidence, only a few mothers leaving their flats pushing children in strollers.

"Well, I did come around to thinking it might have been him that did the murders," Doris said cautiously.

"Good gracious," Uncle Lawrence said. "Do you mean we are escaping from Nigel's murderer? Doris, you didn't tell me there'd be danger. How *did* he know he'd find you with me?" He frowned at Doris.

"I telephoned to Priam's Priory yesterday after I got to London to give a message for Ram. Dickie answered. I didn't say where I was exactly, just with an old friend." She looked sufficiently uneasy, however, suggesting to Margaret that she had indeed said whom she was with.

Uncle Lawrence was still frowning. "And I telephoned to say that when you met me at Harrods, I would be bringing with me a guest who'd come to stay unexpectedly."

"Dickie?" Margaret said suddenly. She looked at her watch again. De Vere must already have arrived to meet her at the flower stand. She prayed that he'd just wait peacefully. "All right, Doris, tell me quickly about you and one Richard Harbert."

"Well, I knew Dickie from back home. He started out working with the gamekeeper at this big house where I had a position. He was a good-looking man, older than me. He didn't like tramping around through the woods in muddy wellies, keeping his eye on the pheasants for the shooting season, so he talked himself into a job in the house, just a footman. But I was surprised, I tell you, to find that he had gone to be the butler at Priam's Priory. I mean, he was always pretending to be grander than he was, and he did learn a thing or two about how to behave like an upper servant. . . . "

"Rather like you were tutored by Nigel," Margaret murmured.

"He wrote to me for a while and told me about the Priory and your family. . . . " She hesitated. "Then I went off to London and never heard from him again. I never thought I'd see him face-to-face, but since I knew all about him, he didn't like the idea that I could tell David."

"Why didn't you tell someone about Nigel's murder?"

"I was afraid," Doris said plaintively, "and I couldn't leave Ram just then. I had to wait until I had the chance to get away. Lady Margaret, Dickie's dangerous. He looks the proper butler, but he's a terror. But when I telephoned, he told me that he was leaving Priam's Priory, so I thought I'd be safe."

"But he's after you," Margaret said impatiently. "You can't have it both ways." Doris was becoming tiresome, and Margaret was finding it difficult to believe anything she said.

"He must have decided that since I know he's a murderer, he has to kill me, too. And then, of course, I have something he wants," Doris said in a small voice. The grand lady with a dubious claim to quasi-royal status had become the frightened prey of a dangerous man.

"What is it exactly that you have?" Margaret asked.

Doris and Uncle Lawrence looked at each other.

"Something that belongs to His Highness," Uncle Lawrence said. "It's worth a great deal of money. Doris has done something quite naughty that I don't approve of, and I have insisted that she return it."

"I don't think it's that simple," Margaret said. "It may have to do with money, but I think it also has to do with a marriage."

Chapter 22

"*We're going* to meet De Vere," Margaret said. "Then we'll go to the Priory immediately, and Doris can return whatever it is she stole from His Highness. Meanwhile, I will tell you what I think, Doris, and you will correct me if I am wrong."

They followed her obediently along the Hans Road exit from Hans Place.

"David said he thought you'd been married," Margaret said.

Doris looked down at the pavement and didn't speak.

"Presumably married to an ambitious Harbert, who would not have been welcome at the Priory with a wife in tow. My mother was still alive in those days, and as old-fashioned as ever. So he came alone—possibly with forged references—leaving a resentful young wife behind in a boring village with only occasional letters describing the splendors of his new position."

"I couldn't stay there forever," Doris said. "I hated it."

"So you looked for a new life in London, without benefit of a divorce. Ram-Sam might be liberal in terms of his own domestic arrangements, but I doubt that he would take kindly to having one of his women married to someone else, and a servant to boot. But I imagine the maharani overheard you and Harbert and grasped the situation. She went off to tell her husband, and she died. Nigel probably knew your secret, and he died."

Margaret was quite pleased with her summary. Doris was nodding as though in agreement.

They were nearing the flower stand, and Margaret breathed a sigh of relief at the sight of De Vere chatting with a newspaper seller on the corner.

Then, on the opposite corner, she saw Harbert. De Vere seemed not to have noticed him, but Harbert had seen him and was waiting for Margaret, for Doris, even for Uncle Lawrence. She had no idea how a desperate man would behave, for surely if he had come looking for one or all of them, he was desperate. Then she had an idea.

"Quickly," she said, "back into the store. We're going to go through and come out on Brompton Road."

They ducked into the store without being seen.

"Wait, Margaret," Uncle Lawrence said. "I think you ought to know what it is that Doris has taken."

"Oh, the money part," Margaret said. "I presume she made off with some valuable jewelry to insure that she could live on comfortably after being replaced by Jazmin Burns."

"Nothing so trivial." Doris reverted to her imperious regal voice. "Nigel and I had planned it for a long time, ever since Mr. Priam here told me about it years ago."

Margaret stopped. "Nigel? It?"

"We called it The Rock," Doris said.

Uncle Lawrence said, "Ram-Sam managed to hang on to things from the Tharpur treasury you couldn't imagine, even after the government took away his privy purse and closed down the princes." He reached into his green Harrods bag and took out an object wrapped in tissue paper. There in the middle of the store, he opened it and showed Margaret the lump of dull glass set in a metal frame that she had seen holding down papers on Ram-Sam's desk. "This is perhaps the most valuable thing he owns."

"Don't tell me," Margaret said faintly. "It's an uncut diamond."

"Part of the old Tharpur treasure," Uncle Lawrence said. "Not widely known. I believe the Nizam of Hyderabad had something like it. When he was a rather foolish young man, His Highness showed it to me and boasted of its value.'' He hesitated. ''And when I became a foolish old man, I liked to tell tales about the past. I spoke of the diamond to Nigel and Doris once when they visited.''

''It would have worked if the maharani hadn't been listening at doors, and if Nigel hadn't gotten greedy,'' Doris said crossly. ''We'd planned it for ever so long.''

Margaret was stunned. ''Do you mean to say that you and Nigel set out to ensnare the maharajah right from the start?''

Doris nodded. ''When Mr. Priam told us about the rock, we started pretending how grand it would be to have it. It wasn't hard to get me introduced to Ram—David didn't know what we were planning—and it didn't take long to come to an arrangement.''

''But how did you find Nigel in the first place?'' Margaret was now reeling.

Doris looked surprised that Margaret found that difficult to figure out. ''I knew about him and David from Dickie. I looked Nigel up in the telephone directory, just for fun. We got on right from the start, and one thing led to another. Once we'd made the plan about the rock, it took a long time to find out where it was. Ram had taken it out of India long ago when the regulations weren't so strict, and put it in a bank in England. So I had to go ahead with living out there in India until we got here and he brought it out to have lying around so he could look at it. I thought we'd be staying in a hotel, and I could just take it, meet Nigel, and disappear.''

''How did Harbert get involved?''

''I needed his help—in exchange for me not telling about us being married and all that. Dickie had keys to everything, so I could get into Ram's rooms when he wasn't there. I didn't tell him exactly what I was trying to take, but Nigel did. He promised him a share. First Her Highness heard Dickie and me talking about everything.''

''So the night of the dinner, when Harbert saw the maharani heading for what she supposed was the place her husband was, he stabbed her. And then he decided to get this . . . this rock for himself, and shot Nigel.''

Doris nodded, as the tourists and shoppers swirled about her.

"We've got to get to De Vere," Margaret said, "and get the diamond safely back to His Highness. Harbert can't take us all on, but we need to be careful. Then we need to do something about capturing him."

"No! He'll go away someplace and never be heard of. I know him."

"Can't let the fellow get away with murder," Uncle Lawrence said. "Wouldn't be right."

"We'll ask De Vere," Margaret said. "Just follow me closely."

They emerged cautiously from Harrods. A black London cab with a solid-looking youngish driver was waiting at the curb directly in front of them.

"Now!" Margaret said, and ran to the taxi. The others followed her as she piled into the broad backseat.

"This is unusual," Margaret said, "but would you be so kind as to drive slowly to the far side of the next street, and pick up a gentleman in blue jeans and a jacket. Unmistakably American."

"Right, miss," the driver said calmly. "And then where?"

"I hadn't thought," Margaret said. "Perhaps a tour of London." She was still absorbing the tale of the fabulous treasure of the maharajah. "There he is, driver." She had spotted De Vere, now looking anxiously about for some sign of her. Harbert was still on the opposite side of the street.

The taxi glided to the curb, and Margaret opened the door. "De Vere! Get in!"

He was startled, but he moved toward the taxi without hesitation. By the time the door was shut, they were already moving into the heavy Brompton Road traffic.

Margaret looked out through the back window. The headlines on the papers displayed by the news seller indicated that Doris had talked in quite a colorful manner about events at the Priory.

The figure of Harbert against the deep red-brown mass of Harrods was growing smaller and smaller.

"What's going on, Margaret?" De Vere asked.

"We have had quite an interesting morning being pursued by Harbert. This is my uncle Lawrence Priam," Margaret said, "and I don't believe you got to meet Doris at the Priory."

De Vere was clearly taken aback.

"Doris Harbert," Margaret added. "It's gotten quite complicated. The butler did it."

De Vere was momentarily speechless. Then he said, "I don't believe that's ever happened in all my years as a policeman. Only in England . . ." He shook his head in amazement.

Margaret leaned forward to speak to the driver. "Could you take us around by Buckingham Palace and Pall Mall, Trafalgar Square and such?" Margaret hoped that during the informal tour, she and De Vere could decide how to bring Harbert to justice, retrieve her car, and get them back to Priam's Priory with the Tharpur diamond. She had a sudden guilty thought. Both Mrs. Domby and Lys were going to be disappointed by the outcome of her venture into Harrods: no supplies to restock the larder, no pretty little gift to win the affections of David's new romantic interest.

"Traffic is something terrible today," the driver said.

"No matter," Margaret said. "Drive where it suits you. We'll be ending up back at Harrods eventually."

"As long as the meter runs and somebody pays the price of the ride . . ." The driver shrugged and drove on.

"Now," Margaret said, "what are we going to do about all this? He wouldn't dare come back to the Priory as though nothing had happened, do you think?"

"He's got cheek," Doris said. "Bold as they come. I wouldn't be surprised if he went back and expected things to go on as before." She was beginning to look a bit worried. "I've been thinking that maybe Mr. Priam here could return the rock, and I'd just go off, and forget everything. Yes, that's the best plan. All Ram cares about is having those millions of pounds back.''

"Wait," De Vere said. "What is *this* about?"

Margaret explained briefly.

"And here I said the maharajah wouldn't leave around anything he couldn't afford to lose."

"He could afford to lose this if he chose," Doris said.

"We're forgetting about Harbert," Margaret said. "Should we capture him in London? Otherwise he might try to escape to the continent like Chloe."

"Margaret," De Vere said firmly. "I am certain the English police would rather not have you rounding up a murderer on your own. Why don't we find a telephone so you can call the Priory. Let Westron and the Scotland Yard people do any capturing that is necessary."

Mrs. Domby answered the telephone, sounding agitated.

"Mr. Westron is right here, Lady Margaret, and I'm sure I don't know what's happening. Potts was supposed to go to London, but he said Harbert went instead. Now, I don't mind that, but Tilda saw him carrying out two suitcases when he left, so I don't know if he's gone on a holiday without telling me. . . . ''

"Let me speak to Mr. Westron," Margaret said.

Westron listened to her, and finally said, "We'll look into Mr. Harbert, Lady Margaret." He did not sound pleased with her heroic efforts to assist the police.

When she returned to the idling taxi, the driver said, "The fare's going up, miss."

She found a handful of five-pound notes. "Drive on," she said. "Back to Beaufort Gardens."

Because Margaret couldn't bear to upset Mrs. Domby further, she and Uncle Lawrence and Doris waited in the car with the engine running while De Vere ventured to Harrods to pick up the order, which was still waiting.

"There's convincing evidence that Harbert has decided to effect his release from employment at Priam's Priory," Margaret said. She hoped that Phyllis Flood would not see this as a golden opportunity to acquire the Priory's butler for Rime Manor. "Now we have to deal with His Highness and the rock Doris stole from him. I'm not looking forward to that.''

Doris looked as though she, too, did not find the prospect entertaining. ''He'll be bloody furious,'' she said. ''But I suppose he can't complain too much if he's got it back.''

Chapter 23

"I want you to be with me," Doris said, "both of you, when I give it back." Doris had been entirely silent and brooding for the trip back from London until they reached the gates of the Priory.

Uncle Lawrence nodded. Margaret was not keen on facing the wrath of the Maharajah of Tharpur. She was also not looking forward to facing the police with her tale.

Mrs. Domby's agitation had subsided.

"I told her I'd already phoned that good London agency for a replacement for Harbert," David said. "I don't think Mrs. Domby and he got on anyhow. The police want to see you."

She faced them alone. Westron was on the brink of departure, and his colleagues were not at all the same rather sympathetic sort he was.

"We frown on the public getting involved in murders," said one. He did not do much to conceal his displeasure.

"We have no proof that this Richard Harbert committed any crime except apparently leaving his position without notice. He could have been offered a better job and decided to chuck this one," said the other.

"Well, of course he is the murderer," Margaret said, but as she spoke, her conviction wavered. Ambitious yes, but did Harbert have the boldness to risk losing what he'd achieved? In spite of what Doris had said about him, Harbert did not strike Margaret as bold. "Who else could it be?" she added weakly. They were hesitating because the proof was lacking. She hesitated now because she saw the murders from a different perspective. They had been daring, risking all to gain all. "At least you must find him and question him."

"We are looking into it, Lady Margaret." This time it was the soothing voice of Westron. She was dismissed.

Late in the afternoon, the Maharajah of Tharpur agreed to receive Mr. Lawrence Priam, Lady Margaret, and his former great and good friend, Doris Harbert.

His Highness's rooms were still in their extreme Indian state. Apparently the police had not yet given him permission to remove himself and his entourage.

"Lawrence, this is a sad meeting for both of us," the maharajah said from his seat on the sofa atop his cushions. "But I am nevertheless pleased to see you. Devi, I am very, very cross."

Unexpectedly Doris flung herself dramatically at his feet, but at least showed enough restraint not to cling to his knees. "Ram, I had to take it. You were going to cast me out. I couldn't start over without anything. You showed me what life could be, and I couldn't face poverty and being alone. Please, please, forgive me."

Margaret thought this a bit much, seeing that she had set out to rob him from the start. She held her tongue, however, curious to see how the scene would play out.

"Give it to me," he said sternly.

"Mr. Priam has it," Doris said meekly. "I didn't want to touch it again."

Uncle Lawrence extracted the ugly but priceless lump of carbon from his Harrods bag and handed it to the maharajah.

"Margaret, this is a very precious piece of my heritage," His Highness said. "I should one day like to tell you its history, but this is not the time. Doris, do stand up."

Doris got to her feet. He opened his gilt box where he kept the things he chose to bestow on ladies. "Take this and go where you will."

Margaret sighed. He was handing her the emerald necklace. Doris had risked a lot by coming back, but she had turned a very substantial profit after all. She had an almost gleeful look as she grasped the necklace. Then she met Margaret's eye, and for a brief moment, she was again the haughty Second Her Highness.

"Go," His Highness repeated. He looked away from her pointedly.

"Wait," Margaret said.

"I'm not waiting, Lady Margaret. I'm going down to London immediately. I want to put all of this out of my mind, that old woman with her bloody handprints on the stones, and your nasty old dog after me in the dark and those ghosts of yours. And you're wrong about them—your two ghosts do haunt the same space—at the same time."

Margaret stared at Doris's back as the implications of what she had said so flippantly took hold.

"Cheerio, Mr. Priam. Thanks for the hideout." Doris stuffed the necklace into her handbag, turned on her heel, and marched out quickly. Uncle Lawrence blinked and looked confused.

"I can't allow this," Margaret said as she headed after Doris. "She practically confessed to me."

Doris was halfway down the big staircase when Margaret caught her. "Doris!"

"Yes?" Doris stopped and turned. She looked cocky and confident, and there was a triumphant gleam in her eye.

"The butler didn't do it," Margaret said. "You did."

Doris tilted her head as she looked back up the ornate staircase and smiled. "Can't prove it."

"You took Highness's dagger from his room, and you murdered his wife to keep her from telling him what she overheard—that you were already married to Harbert, and that you and Nigel were going to steal the diamond. Did you watch the poor dying maharani mark the floor of the Nun's Walk with her handprints?"

Doris tossed her head and turned away.

"Then you dropped the dagger out the window to confuse the police. You got a rifle—is that the help Harbert gave you?—and shot Nigel. Later you tried to shoot me." Doris's expression told her she was right. "You were a country girl whose gamekeeper husband taught her to shoot. Did you and Nigel have a falling out over the diamond? Or was he planning to speak himself to the maharajah?"

Doris shrugged jauntily. "Nigel wanted to split the proceeds from the diamond in half, after we'd given a bit to Dickie. But I was the one who had to live in India and do Ram's bidding for all that time, I had to put up with that hateful woman, and the heat and dust, so I deserved a lot more than half. I still say you can't prove anything."

"Perhaps not right now," Margaret said. "But I know it was you in the Nun's Walk leaving the rifle. I saw the two ghosts, and you saw them, too. Why on earth did you risk coming back?"

Doris laughed. "The diamond is a fake. I took it to a chum in London, the place where Nigel used to sell his father's bits of Indian jewelry. He laughed and laughed. So I decided to bring it back to Ram. I knew he'd give me something worth a lot. He's very generous." She patted her bag. "These are the real thing."

Margaret wondered in passing if Highness was well aware that the stone Doris had taken was a fake. He had not been especially disturbed about his loss when she and De Vere had had their audience. If he couldn't afford to lose the real thing, it was probably still locked safely away.

"Aren't you afraid Harbert will tell someone what he knows about you? Aren't you worried that he thinks you have money from the diamond that you promised him?"

"He doesn't worry me. Now that I've got the necklace, nobody's ever going to find me."

"Why did you shoot at me?"

"You were getting at Dickie," she said. "He was nervous. If you started people thinking about him, he'd weaken. I'm sorry I missed. It would have been much simpler if I hadn't. I do have to go. I fixed it with one of the press boys to watch at the pub for us coming back from London. He's outside on his motorbike to take me off. Maybe I'll even sell him another exclusive story."

She continued down the stairs.

Margaret followed. "You killed my cousin. I won't let you get away with that."

"Then you'll have to move very fast," Doris said at the door. "Because I'll have my press lad throw caution to the winds to get me far, far away. I've taken too many risks to let this slip from me." Doris ran, clutching the bag with her emerald treasure.

Margaret raced to the policemen in the library.

"It was Doris," she said. "She's getting away."

They looked at her.

"She just told me she killed the maharani and my cousin. You must stop her."

A motorbike roared in the drive. When the police and Margaret ran out to the drive, they saw Doris waving gaily from her seat behind the driver as the motorbike sped away.

When they picked up the pieces not much later on the narrow country road, the driver of the motorbike had not been much damaged by the collision with the Floods' Jaguar, but Doris had not been wearing a helmet.

"This has been awful," Margaret said to De Vere as they walked across the meadow to the little rotunda by the lake, trailed by Wally, who had actually attempted to chase a rabbit but had quickly reconsidered.

There had been too much confusion in the house to soothe her, as the maharajah's entourage packed up to move on and Mrs. Domby waged a fierce battle to assume dominance over the new butler.

"I feel a fool for not seeing sooner that the murderer had to be the person who was willing to take the greatest risks."

De Vere hugged her at about the spot where she had jumped into the lake after the rifle shot.

"Too many risks here," he said. "Let's go home."

About the Author

JOYCE CHRISTMAS has written seven previous novels: *Hidden Assets* (with Jon Peterson), *Blood Child*, *Dark Tide*, *Suddenly in Her Sorbet*, *Simply to Die For*, *A Fête Worse Than Death*, and *A Stunning Way To Die*. In addition, she has spent a number of years as a book and magazine editor. She lives in New York City.